CASKET FOR SALE

ONLY USED ONCE

AN ANDREW MAYHEM THRILLER

5 Stars! Highly recommended for totally sick people.
—Detra Fitch, Huntress Reviews

CASKET FOR SALE

ONLY USED ONCE

AN ANDREW MAYHEM THRILLER

JEFF STRAND

(Being the third chronicle in the adventures of Andrew Mayhem)

Mundania Press

A Mundania Press Production

Mundania Press LLC
6470A Glenway Avenue, #109
Cincinnati, Ohio 45211-5222

To order additional copies of this book, contact:
books@mundania.com
www.mundania.com

Cover Art © 2004 by Darrell King
Edited by Rie Sheridan
Book Design and Layout by Daniel J. Reitz, Sr.
Production and Promotion by Bob Sanders

ISBN: 1-59426-350-7

First Trade Paperback Edition • March 2005

Library of Congress Catalog Card Number 2004100306

Production by Mundania Press LLC
Printed in the United States of America

10   9   8   7   6   5   4   3   2   1

Chapter One

If you are reading these words, then I am dead.

Well, okay, maybe not. I guess it's just as likely that some doofus screwed up and sent this out early. So let me clarify: If you're reading these words, I *might* be dead, but there's also a strong possibility that I'm very much alive and extremely annoyed.

Anyway, my name is Andrew Mayhem, and a couple of weeks ago I'd returned to my Florida home following an adventure that can best be described as "really truly seriously totally completely messed up in a big freakin' way." Not to be whiny or anything, but after an experience where you fight for your life against a half-dozen psychopaths and sustain injuries including but not limited to a direct knife hit to the right buttock, is it really so much to ask that the rest of your year be an improvement?

It wasn't gonna happen.

In fact, as I pushed open the wooden doors and walked down the menacing corridor, I knew deep within my soul I was about to face my most terrifying experience yet.

My blood ran ice-cold as I entered Human Resources.

"Have a seat, Mr. Mayhem," said the elderly woman after I introduced myself. "I'm Ms. Bennett."

I almost sighed with pleasure as I sat down. It wasn't an especially comfortable chair, but I'd finally healed enough from the aforementioned buttock injury that sitting was no longer painful, so I was enjoying the experience as much as possible. You don't realize how many times you're required to sit in any given day until you've been stabbed in the rear. And because injuries to that particular region are inherently hilarious, nobody gives you any sympathy. It's a lose-lose situation all around.

While Ms. Bennett looked over my job application, I tried not to fidget. It wasn't the most impressive résumé in the world, but even if none of them lasted more than two or three weeks, the *quantity* of my previous jobs had to count for something, right?

I nervously scratched my cheek, and she noticed my left hand was wrapped in gauze. "Oh, what happened there?" she asked.

"Knife accident," I replied, shrugging it off.

"Really? Did you have to get stitches?"

"Yeah, a few. It's fine, though."

Ms. Bennett held up her thumb. "I had to get three stitches when I cut myself on a soup can lid. How many did you have to get?"

"Twenty-four."

"Twenty-four? My word!"

"Well, twelve on each side."

She set down the papers. "On each side?"

"Yeah, the hunting knife went all the way through my palm. It kind of hurt, but it's okay now. I can move it; it just looks a bit gross. The doctors said it'll be good as new."

"How on earth did you get stabbed through the palm with a hunting knife?"

"Uh, well, this guy did it. He's dead, though."

"He's dead? How did he die?"

"It's a long story. Self-defense...you know how it goes."

Ms. Bennett glanced uncomfortably down at my application, but then tried to force a smile. "So, Mr. Mayhem, have you killed anybody else I should know about?"

"Yeah, a few," I admitted. I could feel the potential success of this job interview draining away.

Her smile vanished. "Seriously?"

"Uh-huh."

"How many other people?"

"Not too many. One guy died of a heart attack while I was threatening him with a piece of a broken plate, but that probably doesn't count. I threw a skull with sharpened fangs at a guy who kidnapped my children, but he shot me first, so I think it's justifiable."

At this point, it was pretty obvious I wasn't getting the job, so I figured, the hell with it. "I poked another guy through the neck with a rib bone, which actually makes two deaths by bone products, an interesting piece of trivia if you're into that kind of thing. One guy died from being stabbed by a booby-trapped gargoyle, another guy died when a pile of fake corpses fell on him, and a lady died from being hit by a box full of really sharp weapons, but in all of those cases my involvement was indirect."

Ms. Bennett was silent for a long moment.

"Anything else?" she finally asked.

"No, that's it. And really, I think you can only count the skull, the rib bone, and the self-defense stabbing of the guy who put the hunting knife through my hand. So I guess I've only killed three people total. I'm surprised you didn't hear about any of this on the news."

"I avoid the news, Mr. Mayhem. Too violent."

"Yeah, I don't blame you. The news sucks."

Ms. Bennett leaned back in her chair. "I'm afraid that with your history of...er, justifiable homicides, this is probably not the best place for you to seek employment."

"I can assure you, I'll try my best not to justifiably kill any of my co-workers," I said, trying to keep things lighthearted.

"I'm sorry, Mr. Mayhem. I'll keep your résumé on file."

After I got into my car, I cursed and smacked my palm (not the stabbed one...I learned that particular lesson the hard way) against the dashboard. I should have taken the interview much more seriously. I'd vowed to "straighten up," as it were. I was thirty-three years old and it was time to finally become a responsible human being. Get a real job. Be a better father and husband. Quit accepting money from strangers to perform tasks that went terribly, terribly, terribly wrong.

Oh well. I'd find a real job soon/eventually. And the lady in Human Resources *had* said she'd keep my résumé on file, right?

I drove away from the building and listened to lousy music on the radio for a few minutes until I noticed red and blue flashing lights in my rear-view mirror. Great. I pulled over, rolled down my window, and tried to think of a good excuse for whatever it was I'd done.

The cop exited his vehicle and hurried over to mine. "Andrew Mayhem?" he asked.

"Yes."

"We've got an APB out for you. I'm going to have to ask you to come with me. It's an emergency."

"Is there a problem?" I asked. Considering the officer had just pulled me over and told me it was an emergency, it was pretty safe to assume there was, in fact, some sort of problem, but I've never claimed to possess intelligence.

"Yes, a big one. Please come with me."

There were several police cars and an ambulance outside of Hector's Subs-N-Suds, a sandwich and beer shop, as we drove up. I've only eaten there once. It was okay, although they were stingy with the black olives and my daughter refused to eat more than a bite of her sub because the roast beef had that weird rainbow sheen thing.

As soon as I got out of the police car, Lieutenant Bruce Frenkle walked over. He'd been promoted from Sergeant last week, and his identical twin brother Tony, who remained a Sergeant, still wasn't speaking to him.

"Andrew! Glad you're here, man."

The cop had briefed me about what was going on during the drive over. I looked over at the restaurant, but I couldn't see anybody through the glass doors. "Are they still in there?"

Bruce nodded. "Yeah, they're hiding. He's not talking anymore, but we haven't seen anything to indicate the situation has changed."

"How's the woman?"

"I think he cut her pretty good."

I winced. Considering what this guy was capable of, though, the woman had little reason to complain. Most of his victims ended up headless.

Bruce put his hand on my shoulder. "You don't have to go in there, you know."

"It would be nice if that were true."

I guess technically it *was* true. The guy inside of Hector's Subs-N-Suds was Ned Markstein, otherwise known as the Headhunter. I don't want to overwhelm you with my past history of encounters with psycho killers, so let's just say the Headhunter was trying to capture me to deliver to another group of psycho killers as part of a fun-filled weekend of Games-o-Death, but he ended up being captured, tortured, and stored in a bathroom while I impersonated him during the games. If you haven't read about my previous wacky adventures, you're just going to have to trust me on some of this.

Now he was holding an innocent woman hostage and demanding I be brought in for a chat. Really, it would've been well within my moral rights to say "No offense, anonymous innocent woman, but I'm staying way the hell out of there!"

Unfortunately, though I may be an irresponsible slacker, I'm not the kind of irresponsible slacker who can stand back and let somebody die like that.

While a cop fitted me with a comfy bulletproof vest, Bruce touched a button on his cell phone. "I'll let him know you're here," Bruce told me.

"I can't believe he's making you use your daytime minutes," I said.

Bruce didn't acknowledge my joke, which didn't bother me because he never acknowledged my jokes. "He's here," he said into the phone. He listened for a moment, nodded, and glanced at me. "He says you can go right in. But you don't really have to do this."

I ignored him and walked over to the front doors.

It's okay, I told myself. *You're not breaking your vow to quit being stupid. This is bravery, not stupidity. This is honorable. Stupidity remains far in your past. You're a smart, responsible individual now.*

I opened the door and walked inside Hector's Subs-N-Suds. The Headhunter stood up from behind a counter at the back of the restaurant, holding a knife to the throat of a young woman with puffy red eyes and a tearstained face. He was wearing orange prison garb and didn't quite have the same look of malicious glee he did when I encountered him before.

He giggled maniacally. "Glad you could make it," he said in a high-pitched voice. "Oh, yes, it's always such a pleasure to see my favoritest friend Andrew!"

"Why are you doing the goofy voice thing? I already know it's an act, remember?"

"Oh, yeah," he said in his normal voice. "Glad you could make it anyway."

"No problem. I'd been wanting to see your new fashion statement. That orange suit really brings out the evil in your eyes."

He sneered. "Aren't you going to ask me to let the woman go?"

I gave a casual shrug, even though sweat was pouring down my sides. I couldn't let him know how nervous I was. "Would you do it?"

"There's only one way to find out."

"Okay. Would you care to let the woman go?"

"Sure. Come over here and take her spot."

I shook my head. "I hope you don't think I came in here just to let you kill me. That would be nutty."

The Headhunter pressed the knife more tightly against the woman's throat. "You want her to die?"

"C'mon, Ned, I know you're not stupid. You kill your hostage and those cops outside will mow you down in about three seconds. Why didn't you just run? You haven't even gone to trial yet, so why go to all the trouble of escaping from prison just for this kind of revenge nonsense?"

"I've gotta be honest with you. The whole 'bring me Andrew Mayhem' thing was only because I got stuck here and needed a way to buy myself some time."

For the briefest of moments I was actually kind of offended. "So, what now?"

"Now? Well, I've had some time to think things over, and revenge nonsense really does sound like a good idea." He shoved the woman out of the way, dropped his knife, and kicked it across the floor toward me. "One-on-one. Let's see what you can do."

I picked up the knife. It had some blood and mustard on it. "I don't want to fight you."

The Headhunter grinned. "This is your chance to beat me fair and square. I don't even have my sword. We'll find out if you're really as tough as you say you are."

"I never said I was tough."

"Yes, you did."

I shook my head. "No, I didn't."

"I'm sure you did."

"Nope. Not something I would say."

The Headhunter looked confused for a moment, and then shrugged. "Either way, it's time for a rematch. This time you don't have your wife to protect you. You and me, Mayhem. You with the knife, me with my bare hands. May the best man win."

We stared at each other.

"You've gotta be kidding me," I said, casually stepping out of the way. A gunshot rang out, shattering the window, and the Headhunter dropped to the ground, screaming and clutching his bleeding leg. Within moments, several cops burst into Hector's Subs-N-Suds, their guns pointed at the fallen kidnapper.

Wow. The Headhunter, a savage serial killer who'd come terrifyingly close to murdering my wife and I, had turned into a complete idiot.

I smiled to myself. If even a lunatic like the Headhunter posed no real threat these days, then my vow to stay out of trouble would be no problem to uphold.

Chapter Two

Six Months Later

Wednesday nights were typically spent hanging out with my friend Roger Tanglen at the Blizzard Room, which was the lamest coffee shop in Florida and possibly the world. Most of our conversation was devoted to the low quality of the coffee. It was a long-running, if pathetic, tradition.

But the Blizzard Room was no more. It had burned to the ground (faulty wiring) last week. We'd actually noticed a few sparks the last couple of times we were there, but thought they were meant to be decorative.

So now we sat in the Java Joint, an upscale, modern coffee shop with tables that didn't wobble if you breathed near them and a menu selection longer than my children's combined Christmas lists.

I took a sip of my cappuccino. "Wow," I said. "It contains heat."

"And the foam doesn't make your tongue numb."

"And the cup actually retains most of the coffee."

We drank in silence for a long moment.

"Now what do we talk about?" I asked.

"I dunno."

We drank in silence for a longer moment.

"We could talk about our relationships," Roger suggested.

"Pass."

"I just don't understand why you don't like her."

"I said, pass."

"C'mon, Andrew, she's a nice person. She's gorgeous, we get along great, and I'm learning more about menstruation than I ever thought possible."

"Don't even joke about that. Your continued emasculation is a serious problem."

"I'm just saying, she's the best thing that ever happened to me. She might be The One."

The horrid creature in question was Samantha. Samantha Tracer. Samantha the Demon Monster from Planet Wretch. He'd met her maybe a month ago, and she'd immediately latched onto him the same way that crab thing latched onto John Hurt's face in *Alien*. I half-expected a phallic-looking extraterrestrial to burst out of his stomach at any moment.

Even though he's a loser like me, Roger dates fairly regularly. He's short, kinda pudgy, losing his hair, and has a big nose, but he's got these beautiful blue eyes (so I'm told, since I'm really not the best judge of beautiful blue eyes) that just about bring women to their knees. I'm taller, have more hair, more muscles, and a nose that's in proportion, but my eyes are a non-bringing-women-to-their-knees dingy brown color. We both dress like slobs.

So I wasn't surprised when Roger started dating Samantha, who is admittedly, for all her life-sucking evil, a blonde bombshell. I was surprised it got so serious so fast. My best friend shouldn't be talking about "The One" after a month of dating, and he *certainly* should not have reached the point where phrases like "we could talk about our relationships" came up in our man-to-man conversations.

"She's not The One."

"She might be," Roger insisted.

"She's not."

"I'm serious, I don't get this. Why don't you like her?"

"Because she's Satan."

"Be more specific. What about her makes her Satan?"

"I don't know, it's just...it's just this Satan-vibe I get from her."

Roger glared at me. "That's not good enough. If you've got a problem with my girlfriend, I want to know what it is. Don't give me this vague Satan-vibe crap. What don't you like about her?"

"She's needy."

"She is *not* needy! She's one of the most independent women I know! And I've dated plenty of needy women you've liked. C'mon, Andrew, you've gotta do better than that."

I sighed and took a drink of my coffee. The honest truth is I didn't know *why* I disliked Samantha so much. It was a purely emotional response, based on nothing I could describe, but I wanted her out of my and Roger's life.

"She has head lice," I said.

"Damn it, Andrew, you're really starting to piss me off. Do you want me to stop seeing her? Is that what you want?"

"Yes, please."

"Well, it's not gonna happen, so you'd better get over whatever issues you've got with her. You're supposed to be happy for me. You've got a wife and kids. Maybe that's what I want, too."

"I don't think she has child-bearing hips."

"Okay, you know what, you seem pretty determined to be an asshole tonight. I'll talk to you tomorrow." Roger pushed back his chair, got up, and walked out of the Java Joint, leaving his obscenely overpriced coffee behind.

Fine. If he wanted to continue with that fatality-laden train wreck of a relationship, he could do whatever he wanted. He could marry her for all I cared. Have six or seven hellspawn. But when he came crawling back to me, shriveled and burnt and coughing up flames, I'd just invite him to pucker up those scorched lips and kiss my—

"Hi," said a woman, sliding into the seat Roger had just vacated.

"Uh, hi," I responded. She looked to be in her early twenties, with flowing black hair draped over her shoulders, lipstick a good six shades too red, and sexy wire-framed glasses.

"You look lonely."

"No, I'm fine."

"Just so you know, I'm not here to hit on you. You're Andrew Mayhem, right?"

"Yeah."

"I have a proposition for you."

"No," I said.

"Hear me out. I'm willing to offer you—"

"No."

"It's a lot of—"

"No."

"But—"

"Nooooo," I said, singing the word.

"I don't think you—"

"No, no, no, nope, *nein*, nix, negative, *nyet*, *non*, *nada*, *nein*...I already said *nein*, didn't I?...no, no, no. No."

"*Nada* means 'nothing.'"

"Same difference."

The woman frowned. "May I ask why you're turning me down?"

"You may."

"Why?"

"Because these days I'm a responsible citizen. I no longer accept money from strange women in coffee shops to do things that end up getting me almost killed. Twice I've done it, and twice I've regretted it. I'm done with that. You're looking at the new, improved—"

"One hundred thousand dollars," said the woman.

I tried to say *nada*, but the word stuck in my throat.

"One hundred thousand dollars to deliver a suitcase."

Don't ask what's in the suitcase, I silently pleaded with myself. *Don't ask what's in the suitcase. Don't ask what's in the suitcase.*

"What's in the briefcase?" I asked, overcoming my mental pleading on a technicality.

"You don't need to know."

"Where do you want it delivered? Antarctica?"

"Arizona."

"That's pretty far."

"It's for a hundred thousand dollars."

Do not, under any circumstances, accept this offer. This one deserves the big N-O. Run screaming out of the coffee shop with your hands over your ears if you have to, but do not, I repeat, do not, I repeat again, do not agree to deliver this briefcase. Don't do it. Really.

"I can't," I said, momentarily surprised that I listened to common sense. It felt kind of neat.

The woman stared at me for a long moment, and then shrugged. "Have it your way."

"I will. But I appreciate the offer."

She nodded and left. I took a sip of my coffee, enjoying the feeling of being an intelligent, responsible—

Holy crap, I just turned down a hundred grand, what the hell is wrong with me?

—adult.

This was the new Andrew Mayhem. The most responsible guy on the block. The guy you'd call if you needed somebody to hold your ladder steady while you changed a light bulb. The guy who always had jumper cables in the trunk of his car. Even my Christmas cards were going to be on time this year.

Now if only I could talk some sense into Roger, everything would be perfect.

⁂

The next day, I drove home from work whistling a merry tune. I'd held my job in the mailroom of a heartless corporation run by sinister men in dark suits for over three months now, and today at lunch my boss' boss had nodded and half-smiled in my direction. My future was looking bright.

I opened the front door of my two-story suburban home and saw my children crouched on the floor, their backs to me. They were very excited about something. Something that was snorting.

"Is there a pig in the house?" I asked, shutting the door behind me.

"Daddy!" shouted Theresa, getting to her feet and rushing over to give me a great big hug. She was nine and going through an Affectionate Phase. Now, she'd always been an affectionate child, but these days she'd hug you while you were walking up stairs. She'd even taken to hugging her little brother *without* the intent of crushing him to death.

Kyle, my seven-year-old, stayed crouched on the floor, petting what I saw was not, in fact, a member of the swine family but rather a dog. A pug. One of those tiny flat-faced bug-eyed curly-tailed wrinkly-foreheaded things. It snorted happily.

"Why is there a pug in our house?" I asked.

"That's Joe," Theresa informed me.

"Hi, Joe. Why is there a pug in our house?"

"He's mine!" Theresa said with a big grin.

"He's mine, too!" Kyle shouted.

"Is not!"

"Mom said you could only keep him if we shared!"

"We're keeping him?" I asked. "He's a permanent pug?"

Theresa nodded. "Uh-huh."

Joe snorted some more.

"Where's your mother?"

"Upstairs. See, Misty is moving, and she said she'd have to get rid of Joe and maybe even put him in the pound, and she asked if I wanted him, and Misty's mom brought him over and Mom said we could keep him."

"He's mine, too!" Kyle insisted.

"Shut up. I didn't even say anything about that!"

"Well, he *is*!"

"No duh, stupid."

"Don't call your brother stupid," I said. "And don't tell him to shut up. And isn't Misty that kid who always shoved paste in her ears?"

"It was Play-Doh."

Joe continued to snort.

"Is he supposed to be that ugly?" I asked.

"He's not ugly, he's cute."

The pug, released from Kyle's petting grip, hurried over and began to sniff my feet, snorting all the while. I reached down to scratch his head. I'd always liked dogs, although my tastes ran in the direction of big manly dogs instead of tiny little porcine ones.

"I'm going upstairs to talk to your mother," I announced.

"She doesn't feel good."

"Obviously."

I walked upstairs and down the hall into our bedroom. Helen was sitting in bed, on top of the covers, propped up against a couple of pillows.

"There's a pug in our house," I told her.

"I know."

"The kids said you said they could keep it."

"I know we should've discussed it first, but it's okay, isn't it?"

I shrugged. "It's fine. I just kind of figured we'd consult each other in pug acquisition decisions."

Helen was looking somewhat pale. She's an adorable, petite woman with long brown hair and freckles, who despite her small size has an aura of scary strength about her. But at the moment that aura wasn't present.

"I'm sorry," she said, looking as if she were near tears.

"No, no, it's fine. No big deal. I mean, you usually make the parental decisions anyway. Theresa said you're not feeling very good...what's wrong?"

"It's hard to explain."

What could it be? The flu? Guilt? Menopause two decades early?

"Are you okay? Do I need to call a doctor?"

She shook her head. "Actually, it's not hard at all to explain. Andrew, I'm pregnant."

Chapter Three

"Ah," I said.

Let me give you a bit more information than you probably want to know about the creation of my offspring. Theresa was conceived during our honeymoon. Forms of birth control used at the time: The Pill and condoms (ribbed, but without spermicidal lubricant). The condom broke while The Pill was on its lunch break, and whammo...Helen was pregnant with our daughter.

Kyle was conceived two years later, when Helen's parents took Theresa for the weekend. We had a lovely, romantic dinner where we discussed how nice it was just being the two of us for a change, a comment that obviously had Fate cackling with malicious glee. Forms of birth control used at the time: The Pill, condoms (with spermicidal lubricant), a diaphragm, and through coincidence, the rhythm method.

After the birth of Kyle, Helen decided that perhaps she was remarkably prone to pregnancy, and suggested a more effective solution than all of our previous attempts at birth control combined. I spent three weeks whimpering, coming up with excuses, and keeping my legs defiantly crossed, but finally relented and underwent the dreaded V-word.

"I swear I didn't cheat on you," Helen said, a tear trickling down her face.

"I know."

"There's a less than one percent chance of a vasectomy failing, but it does happen. And you know there were complications..."

"Please don't talk about the complications."

"We could do a test if you really wanted to be sure."

I climbed onto the bed and sat next to her. She leaned against me and put her arms around me, now crying openly.

"Sweetie, I trust you completely," I said, meaning it.

"I just got so scared when I found out...I thought maybe you wouldn't believe me..."

"I believe you."

She looked up at me, eyes glistening. "Are you sure?"

"One hundred percent."

"Thank you so much."

We just sat there, holding each other for several minutes. Helen's sobs subsided, and she wiped her eyes off on her shirt. Then she smiled. "So are you happy about it?"

Now we had entered the ultimate danger zone. The mother of all trick questions. I had voluntarily allowed somebody to slash at my testicles with a scalpel, and now I was being asked if I was pleased it had been for naught.

However, it was the same question I'd been asked when the birth control pills and condoms failed, twice, and though I'm far from the most intelligent guy on the planet I'm also not usually a complete idiot.

"Of course I am."

She hugged me tighter. "I'm so glad. I love you."

"I love you too," I said, since it was a more politically wise thing to say than the "Oh, *shiiiiiiit!*" I was thinking.

I knew what had caused this. It was Roger's sudden desire for children. That bastard's brain waves had infiltrated my scrotum, reconnecting my vas deferens and causing me to impregnate my wife, allowing him to vicariously experience the joys of new fatherhood. I was going to kick his ass the next time I saw him.

"How far along are you?" I asked.

"Five weeks."

We were silent for a moment, each of us lost in thought.

Andrew Mayhem, father of three.

Dear Lord.

"So," I said, "do you think the pug will like the new baby?"

⁊⁊

We went downstairs to find Kyle and Joe playing tug-of-war with one of my best clip-on ties. "Hey, knock it off."

"Joe started it."

"Don't blame the pug." I tried to get my tie back, but Joe wasn't about to give it up without a fight, so I let it go. Joe looked at me, clearly annoyed that I'd ended the game after such a feeble attempt, and barked.

"Zip it," I told him.

Joe snorted some more.

"Your mother and I have a family announcement to make, so everybody gather on the sofa," I said. We all sat down on the sofa, joined by Joe.

"Are we going on vacation?" asked Theresa.

"No."

"Aw."

"I wanna go to Stinky Blinky's World," said Kyle.

"Too bad, that's not what this announcement is about. Are you ready?"

Theresa and Kyle nodded.

"I'm going to have a baby," Helen told them, beaming.

"Yay!" Kyle shouted.

"I thought Daddy was snipped," said Theresa.

Helen looked simultaneously horrified and way-too-amused. "Theresa!"

"You said he was, that one time when I asked why I couldn't have a baby sister."

"Why are you telling her these things?" I asked Helen. "What's wrong with the stork?"

"Daddy, I'm nine," said Theresa. "Duh."

"What was snipped?" Kyle asked.

"Nothing," I told him. "They're both crazy in the head."

Kyle twirled his index finger in a circle around his ear.

"I thought that since Daddy was snipped, you couldn't have a baby," said Theresa.

"The doctors didn't snip hard enough," Helen informed her.

"Were their scissors dull?"

"All right, *enough!*" I demanded. "You kids go walk the dog. I don't like the way he's sniffing the carpet."

Finding the leash and putting it on Joe was a tremendous but unsurprising ordeal, but finally my children went out the front door. I sank back into the couch. My stomach hurt.

"Are you sure you're happy?" Helen asked.

"Quite."

"You know, taking a vacation really isn't a bad idea. We haven't taken a family vacation in over a year, the kids are out of school for the summer, and this may be our last chance for a while. We could rent a motor home and do some camping."

"That sounds like fun."

"If you wanted we could even invite Roger and Samantha."

I stiffened. "What do you mean, Roger and Samantha?"

"What's wrong with that?"

"Why is Samantha automatically included? You make it sound like they're a couple."

"Aren't they a couple?"

"No, they're just dating. There's a difference. They aren't 'Roger and Samantha' yet."

"I don't understand why you don't like her."

"It doesn't matter."

"She's very nice."

"Can we talk about something else?" I asked. "Here, let's chat about my failed snipping again. Remember that one time I had a vasectomy and you still got pregnant? I thought I was gonna laugh myself into a seizure over that one."

Helen stood up. "If you don't want to do the vacation thing, that's all right. I just thought we could use some fun, that's all."

"No, you're right, you're absolutely right. Let's do it. We'll camp out, roast marshmallows and weenies, sing campfire songs, feed our children to bears if they get out of hand...it'll be great!"

Helen grinned. "Why don't you give Roger a call to see if he can get the time off?"

"Sounds good." I gave her a kiss, went into the kitchen, picked up the phone, and dialed Roger's number. He answered on the fourth ring. "Hey, how's it going?" I asked.

"Hi," he said, sounding distant.

"You okay?"

"I'm fine."

I frowned. "Are you still mad at me?"

"Shouldn't I be?"

"Do you see what she's done to you? You're still mad! You never would've still been mad before!" Roger and I argued all the time, and the extent of our reconciliation had always been an exchange or two of the word "Dude." This vile menace needed to be stopped. Roger's sanity depended on it.

"I'll call you later," he said.

"No, no, hold on a second," I said. "I was calling to invite you on a camping trip. You and Samantha. Both of you."

"Really? When?"

"Soon. Whenever you can get off work."

"Well, I can get off work anytime, but I'll have to check with Samantha."

Maybe everything would work out. Maybe Samantha wouldn't be able to take time off from her job (she did something with clothing, or maybe it was seafood) and Roger would be free of her foul tentacles for a week or so. That might be long enough to break her mental grip. Perfect!

⁊❧

As is typical in my life, things did not work out perfectly. Samantha was willing and able to take a few days off from whatever she did with clothing or seafood, and a week later I found myself behind the wheel of a gargantuan motor home, Roger in the passenger seat, Helen, Samantha, Theresa, Kyle, and Joe in the back. Helen and Samantha were playing cards. Theresa and Kyle were playing "Strangle the Sibling." Joe was snorting.

We'd left early in the morning and were on our way to Wreitzer Park in Georgia, which Samantha had highly recommended. I could only assume this meant it was laden with rattlesnakes, tarantulas, locusts, and second-tier demons, but both Helen and Roger thought it sounded great so I relented.

Helen and I had originally decided to wait until after the camping trip to share the news that she was pregnant. However, we then realized the secret was already known by Theresa and Kyle, two individuals with a poor track record in the secret-keeping business, and so we told Roger and Samantha as soon as we'd finished packing the camper.

Samantha squealed with delight and threw her arms around Helen. Roger looked confused.

"I thought you had a vasectomy," he whispered.

"I did. It didn't take. I'm so darn masculine that even a ghastly medical procedure can't stop my tadpoles from swimming." I flexed my muscles and growled.

As we crossed the border from Florida into Georgia, we stopped the camper at a rest area and each had a ceremonial peach. The kids went off to walk the pug while the women headed for the restroom.

"This is nice," said Roger, cracking open a Mountain Dew. "I don't know why we don't take vacations like this more often."

I stretched my arms over my head and yawned. "You're right. I think we need to schedule at least one non-psycho-killer-related vacation a year."

"Deal."

Roger was silent for a moment, and I was sure he was going to make some unwanted comment about his relationship with Samantha. But he didn't, thank goodness. However, a couple of minutes later his eyes lit up as he saw her walking back toward the camper.

"How're you holding up with the driving?" she asked me when she returned. She was holding an assortment of six chocolate bars she'd bought from the vending machine.

"Fine. I'm enjoying it, actually."

Okay, I'll be honest with you. Samantha was absolutely stunning. She had long, curly blonde hair, an awesome figure, and a killer smile. Of course, since she was probably able to take on other forms at will, why *not* pick one that was physically attractive?

(You know, it just occurred to me that some of you may be reading this and thinking I'm some kind of aluminum foil-wearing freak. So let me clarify that despite my numerous comments, I didn't *really* believe Samantha was Satan, an alien, or a shape-shifting beast. It's just my sense of humor. Really. I apologize for any confusion.)

Samantha flashed me her killer smile and tossed me a candy bar. "Energy for the road."

"Thanks."

I should also share that Samantha didn't know how I felt about her. At least Roger claimed never to have told her ("She doesn't need to know you're an idiot.") and she certainly didn't act like she knew.

The children returned and Samantha provided each of them with a candy bar as well. Nothing like sugared-up elementary school-age kids to add some excitement to a road trip, but hey, I wasn't sitting back there with them.

When Helen got back, we piled into the motor home and resumed our drive. It was uneventful until twenty minutes later, when Samantha walked up and leaned behind us.

"You can get off at this exit," she said.

"That's not what the map says," I told her.

"I know. This is a shortcut."

"No shortcuts."

"It'll save us about half an hour."

"I don't care. We're sticking with the map. I no longer accept money from strange women in coffee shops, and I certainly don't take surprise shortcuts."

"She's good with directions," Roger insisted.

I glared at him. "Do you remember being locked in a cage to be hunted for sport?"

"Yeah, but that was because we accepted money from a strange woman in a coffee shop, not because we took a shortcut."

"No shortcuts."

"That's fine," said Samantha. "No big deal."

"Thank you."

Samantha returned to the main part of the camper.

"That was pretty rude," said Roger.

"No shortcuts."

Fifteen minutes later, we arrived at the map-approved exit.

Fifteen minutes after that, we were driving down a narrow, creepy dirt road through the woods that sort of made me wish we'd taken the shortcut.

Chapter Four

A run-down, barely standing store had a faded sign that read "Last Chance 4 Gas." (The word "chance" was barely visible, but identifiable through context clues.) Fortunately, our gas tank was seven-eighths full. There would be no running out of gas in sinister locations during this trip. No way.

"Joe needs to go potty," said Theresa.

"You just walked him at the rest area."

"He needs to go again. He's walking funny."

"Okay, fine." I pulled the camper into what passed for the parking lot. There were no other cars, not even one for whoever worked there. Maybe nobody did.

"I'm going inside," said Roger, getting out of the vehicle.

"Why? Do you have to go potty too?"

"I want to check the expiration date on their beef jerky. I'm guessing late eighties."

"Doesn't it hurt to be such a geek?" I asked.

"You can't say you aren't curious. Samantha, Helen, you coming with us?"

"I think we're fine," said Helen.

"We'll send a search party in ten minutes," Samantha added.

Roger and I walked inside the store, careful not to slam the door and cause the entire structure to come crashing down to the ground. The aisles were narrow, the scent was interesting, and an elderly man sat behind the front counter, glowering at us as he paged through a tattered sports car magazine.

"Got any beef jerky?" Roger asked.

The old man coughed. "Yeah, but you don't wanna eat it."

"I'll trust you on that one," said Roger, looking through the candy rack for unusual and ancient selections. I noticed the magazines on the rack were at least a year old, unless a certain celebrity had gotten re-married and re-divorced without my hearing about it.

"Where're you headed?" asked the old man.

"Wreitzer Park," I told him, looking uncomfortably at a doughnut that had cherry filling leaking from the side with an ant imbedded in it, like those fossilized bugs in amber.

"Not the safest place to be."

"Really?"

The old man nodded. "Bad elements there."

"What kind of bad elements?"

"Dangerous ones." He coughed. "Deadly ones." He coughed again. "You don't want to be anywhere near Wreitzer Park, trust me on this."

I stared at him, trying to figure out if he possessed great wisdom or great senility.

"What kind of bad, dangerous, and deadly elements?" I asked.

"Just stay away from Wreitzer Park." He returned his attention to the magazine.

"Got it."

"I bet these M&M's are worth something in the collector's market," said Roger, taking them off the rack. He bought the candy, along with a spooky pickle, and we left the store.

"I think we should camp someplace else," I told him.

"Why?"

"Because a creepy old man just told us there are deadly elements there. That, to me, is a good reason to find another place to camp."

"Aw, c'mon, Andrew. He was a nutcase."

"Yes, but nutcases are often the best people to trust."

"Samantha said this park is an abandoned paradise. Nobody ever goes there! We'll probably have the entire place to ourselves!" Roger considered that. "Hmmmm, maybe that's why the dangerous elements decided to go there."

"At the very least we're going to tell Helen and Samantha about it. If we *do* go to that park and something bad happens, I don't want them finding out later we didn't heed some creepy old man's warning."

Theresa and Kyle were helping Joe run in circles around a tree, so Roger and I approached the women.

"Slight problem," I said. "Apparently Wreitzer Park has bad elements."

"Meaning?" asked Samantha.

"I don't know. It was a vague warning. Something about it being deadly."

"I see."

"I'm not necessarily saying we *should* find another camping option, I just wanted to point out there's been a warning about our current plan of action, and if there *are* other options readily available, maybe we should consider them."

"What exactly did you hear?" asked Samantha.

"The old man is right inside. Go in there and tell him where we're going."

The women exchanged a confused look.

"So, you're saying we should go someplace else?" asked Helen.

"Yes."

"Roger?"

"I'm sticking with the 'Looney Old Man Babbling Nonsense' theory, myself."

"I'm not suggesting we cancel the whole trip," I insisted. "I'm just saying that if our choice of parks has been classified as deadly, that maybe we should pick another one that *hasn't* been classified as deadly, that's all. It's not like there aren't other parks. It's, what, one o'clock? We've got plenty of time to find another place. What do you say?"

"If you're really not comfortable going there, then yeah, we should find another place," said Samantha. "We've got the Georgia guide, I'll look through our options while we head back to the highway. What do you think, Helen?"

"I'm fine with it if everybody else is."

"I think it's kinda stupid," said Roger. "But I got my antique M&M's, so we can do whatever you want."

"Great," I said. "Let's get out of here."

We called the kids back to the camper, started the engine, and pulled out of the parking lot, heading back the way we came. Yeah, I felt like a total wuss, but total wusses tend to stay alive. I had my children and pregnant wife with me, and I wasn't going to take any chances whatsoever with their safety.

"He probably just wanted the best fishing spot for himself," said Roger.

"Probably."

"I have to wonder if perhaps you're taking this responsibility thing a bit too far. Maybe there's, you know, a middle ground."

"I *am* on the middle ground," I said. "I could have us all wearing life preservers."

"I guess you're right."

"Wreitzer Park didn't sound all that great anyway. I hear it's over-run with earwigs."

Roger shrugged. "Yeah, but apparently Joe back there is a fear-less earwig hunter."

I was silent for a long moment. "We have some dumb-ass conver-sations, don't we?"

"This was a conversation?"

We'd backtracked about two miles before Theresa and Kyle started to fight over the final chocolate square from one of their candy bars. Theresa claimed she'd been saving it for future consumption, while Kyle's counter-argument was that he, not Theresa, had been the one with the foresight to ration his chocolate, and the final square con-tained his personal tooth marks on the edge as evidence of his deci-sion.

"One of you is lying, and they'd better 'fess up," Helen said, using the version of her don't-mess-with-me voice she directed at children,

which was substantially less frightening than the version she directed
at husbands.

"It's mine!" Kyle insisted.

"Should we pull over for DNA testing?" asked Samantha.

Helen gave Samantha her please-don't-encourage-my-easily-
encouragable-children look.

"I think the store had a DNA test by the jar of pickled eggs," said
Roger.

Helen gave the same look to Roger.

I was smart enough to keep my mouth shut.

"Give me the chocolate," Helen ordered, holding out her hand.

"But it's *mine!*" said Kyle.

"I don't care. If you're going to fight over it, nobody gets the chocolate."

"But then she gets her whole candy bar and I don't get all of mine
because she's a *liar!*"

"I am not!"

"Are too!"

"Am not!"

"Are too, asshole!"

Whoa! Kyle's first curse word. I was glad to be there for a truly
memorable parental moment. I stopped the camper and turned around
in my seat, not wanting to miss this.

"*What* did you say?" Helen demanded.

Kyle looked surprised and terrified, as if the word had escaped
from his mouth without his consent. "Nothing," he said in a small
voice.

"*What* did you say?" Helen demanded again. It seemed peculiar
to want him to repeat a word he was in big trouble for saying in the
first place, but I wasn't about to call her on that.

"He said the a-word," Theresa pointed out, helpfully.

"You be quiet," Helen told her.

"But he did!"

"I know what he said."

"Then why did you ask?"

"All right, I've had *enough* of this! I don't want to hear a *single*
word out of *either* of you until we get to the campground. If I hear *one*
word, even *one*, you will *both* be in more trouble than you can *imagine!*"

Theresa and Kyle sat back in their seats to glare at each other.

I resumed driving.

Vague threats like "more trouble than you can imagine" really
weren't Helen's style. She was usually capable of describing potential
punishments in such minute detail they seemed to be the work of
weeks of preparation. I wondered if she was genuinely shaken up by
this third pregnancy.

"See, Roger, all of this could be yours," I said.

Roger just grinned. To be perfectly honest, though my children drove me absolutely bonkers on a regular basis, I really had gotten a good deal, considering what they'd been through. It had only been about two years since Kyle and Theresa were kidnapped and almost killed. It was my fault, the direct result of a horrific mess Roger and I had gotten ourselves into. Theresa recovered fine, but Kyle had spent a year going to a school for emotionally disturbed children.

That said, most of the time he was a perfectly happy little kid, and if the worst we had to deal with was him calling his sister an asshole, Helen and I were extremely fortunate.

We rounded a corner, and then I applied the brake. A large dark-green truck was stopped in the center of the road, about fifty feet ahead, blocking our path.

"What's he doing?" asked Roger.

"I don't know." The truck was filthy, the front grille covered with unidentifiable gook. I could see that somebody was in the driver's seat, but he didn't appear to be moving.

We waited for about ten seconds.

"Honk at him," Roger said.

"I'll decide when to use the horn, thank you very much," I told him. I gave the horn a light tap.

The truck didn't budge. The driver didn't even react.

"I don't think his engine's on," said Roger.

Samantha moved up to the front and looked through the windshield. "What's up with this guy?"

"Is he awake?" Roger asked.

"Yeah, his eyes are open," said Samantha. "Honk at him again."

"*I* will make all decisions about the use of the horn." I waited for several seconds to prove I was making the decision on my own, and then honked at the truck again.

No response.

"Jeez, I hope he didn't have a heart attack or something," I said, putting the camper into park. "Everybody wait here, I'll go see what the deal is."

I got out of the vehicle and walked toward the truck. The engine was on. The driver was a guy in his late thirties or early forties, with at least a week's worth of beard growth and unkempt long black hair. As I got closer to his truck, it was clear that he was very much conscious and watching me closely.

But as I walked up to the driver's side of the truck, he stared forward, watching the camper. "Hi there," I said, waving to get his attention.

No reaction.

"Hello? Sir?"

Nothing.

What was wrong with this guy? I hesitated for a moment, and then knocked on the door. "Sir?"

He didn't move.

Now, I could tell the guy was watching me when I approached the truck, so why was he ignoring me now? "Sir, I really need for you to move your truck over a bit. We can't get around you."

Again, no response. Now I was starting to get irritated. I knocked on the door again, harder this time. "Hey! I need you to move the truck, okay?"

Very slowly, the man turned his head to look at me. He narrowed his eyes, and then very slowly returned his attention to the camper.

I got ready to pound on the door, but decided that perhaps this was a gentleman I didn't want to make mad. Did I really want to piss off a guy who was acting this strange, and who could easily have a shotgun resting on his lap?

We could always return to our original plan and drive back the way we'd been going before the wimp-out. Of course, there wasn't nearly enough room on the road to turn the camper around until we reached the store. I wasn't quite comfortable enough driving the motor home to relish the idea of driving in reverse for three miles, but what was I gonna do, throw open the door and drag this idiot out of his truck?

I knocked once more. "Sir? Is something wrong? Do you need me to get help?"

He looked over at me and rolled down his window. "Quit touching my goddamn truck." He said these words in a surprisingly articulate manner.

"Sorry about that, but you're in the way."

"What way?"

"The way of my camper. We need to get past you and you're in the middle of the road."

"No kidding."

"Uh, right. So could you move?"

The man opened his door and slowly climbed out of the truck. He was wearing filthy blue jeans and a t-shirt bearing the faded slogan "Quality Counts!" He was tall, at least six-two, and lean but muscular. He had an ID badge clipped to his pants pocket, which featured his picture and the word "Goblin."

"You can't go down that road," he informed me.

"Yes, I realize that. That's what I've been saying. Your truck is in the way."

"I *know* my truck is in the way."

I wanted to grab him by the shoulders, give him a good shaking, and scream "Then *move* it!" but wisely refrained. "Okay, well, since we're both aware of that, maybe you could move it? Just a bit?"

"A tree fell, about a mile up ahead. It's blocking the road. It's right as you go around a corner, and I didn't want you to crash into it."

"Oh. Well, that's very nice of you. Maybe we could help you move it."

The man (Goblin?) shook his head. "The tree's too big."

"We have a couple of people in the camper who could help," I said. Technically, Helen wasn't nearly far enough in her pregnancy to be exempt from manual labor, but regardless, I wasn't going to let her engage in any. "It's just a tree, right? We should be able to get it off the road."

"Nope."

"C'mon, four people should be able to move a tree." Actually, never having moved a tree in my life, I had no idea how much manpower was required, but none of the trees close to the road seemed anywhere near large enough to provide much difficulty.

"What did I just tell you? It's too big of a project. Go back the way you came."

"There's nowhere to turn around."

"That's not my problem. You bringing an oversized vehicle into this narrow road doesn't constitute an emergency on my part."

Clearly, I wasn't going to get this guy to move. "All right, well, thanks for not letting us crash into the tree."

"Not a problem."

Goblin got back in his truck while I returned to the camper. "What'd he say?" asked Roger as I shut the door.

"He says there's a fallen tree blocking the road, and we have to turn back."

"So why was he just sitting in his truck like that?"

"Because he's an extremely odd individual. I think his name is Goblin, by the way."

"Goblin?"

"That's what his badge said."

Roger stuck out his lip in a mock pout. "Everybody else gets all the cool names."

I turned around and spoke to Helen. "I'm gonna have to drive backwards until we get to the store, so I'll need you to watch through the window and let me know if I'm getting too close to the side of the road."

"I'll watch, too!" said Kyle, excited.

"What did I tell you about talking?" asked Helen. "Not one word!" She got up and walked to the back of the camper to look out the rear window. Samantha opened one of the side windows and stuck out her head.

I put the camper in reverse and slowly applied the gas. This really sucked. Stupid store owner and his stupid warning. This was my punishment for being responsible.

"You're okay on my side," Samantha announced as we backed up.

"Yeah, you're fine," said Helen. "Just keep going straight and...oh, crap, someone's coming."

In the side-view mirror I saw a truck drive up behind us. A filthy dark-green truck identical to the one in front. It continued moving toward us until it was no longer visible in the mirror.

"The jerk stopped two inches from our rear!" Helen informed everybody.

Then the truck in front of us began to move, driving forward until it was practically touching the front of our camper.

We were boxed in.

Chapter Five

"Everyone just stay calm," I said as I turned off the camper's engine. "They've got identical trucks, so they're probably just part of the same...I don't know, fallen tree warning squad or something. Helen, what's the guy in the back doing?"

"Nothing. He's just sitting there."

"Does he look homicidal?"

"Not really."

"Good."

I honked at the truck in front of us, trying to get Goblin to back up. He didn't move.

"Okay, let's just wait and see what they want," I said.

We all sat there for a moment, trapped between the two trucks, waiting for something to happen. The drivers just stayed in their vehicles, silently watching us.

"Do you want me to get out?" Roger finally asked.

I shook my head. "Helen, make sure the kids aren't near the windows."

"I'm scared," said Theresa.

"You don't have to be scared, honey," I assured her. "It's just that these people are acting kind of goofy, that's all. Everything will be fine, I promise."

Samantha picked up her purse and reached inside. "I think we should call the police."

"Good idea," said Roger. What a brownnoser.

Samantha took out her cell phone and punched a couple of buttons. "Damn it! The battery's dead. Roger, I thought you said it was charged!"

"I plugged it in last night!" Roger insisted.

"Did you plug it in right?"

"Yes, I plugged it in right. I'm pretty sure I did. I don't know. I've never plugged one in before. I don't like cell phones."

Helen got her own purse and retrieved her cell phone. She looked at the display in disbelief. "My battery's dead, too!"

"Are you serious?" I asked.

"No." Helen gave a half-smile and dialed.

Something else Helen never did was joke during moments of stress. I got in trouble all the time for doing that. This personality change was starting to become scary.

A few seconds later, Helen's half-smile disappeared. "I'm not getting a signal."

"Nothing?" Samantha asked.

Helen held up the display for her to see then tried again. "No signal. It's not working."

"How can that be?" I asked. "We're not that deep in the woods, are we?"

"Maybe the camper's too tightly insulated or something," said Helen.

I frowned. "A camper wouldn't block cell phone reception, would it?"

"I don't know!" Helen snapped. "I'm just saying it isn't working! Where's your phone?"

"It's...I left it at home," I admitted. "It's on the counter. Next to the spatula." I'd only owned the stupid thing for three weeks, and I avoided its use as much as possible.

"Damn it, Andrew, I thought you were going to try to be more responsible!"

I couldn't believe this. "I *am* being more responsible! Look, the gas tank is almost full! I turned away from Wreitzer Park on the word of a crazy old man! So I forgot my cell phone...we had two others in the camper! If you're going to get mad at somebody, get mad at Roger! He forgot to plug in Samantha's phone!"

"It was a funky plug!" Roger insisted.

"Then you should have asked!" Samantha said.

"It looked like it was working!"

"Stop fighting!" Theresa shouted. "You're acting like babies!"

All of the adults shut up. Yes, a nine-year-old who only a short time earlier had been at war over a tiny block of tooth-marked chocolate had successfully put us in our place.

"Let's get the kids out of the way," I suggested, quietly.

Samantha took Kyle's hand. "Here, Kyle, why don't you come up and snuggle with your Aunt Samantha in the top bunk?"

When did she become "Aunt Samantha?" That woman didn't get to appoint herself an honorary aunt without my permission! Who did she think she was? Dear God, if Roger stuck with her he would be whipped beyond all reasonable human—

I put that out of my mind and focused on much more pressing matters, such as, say, the lunatic truck drivers. Samantha helped Kyle onto the upper sleeper, and then climbed up there with him, while Helen huddled down with Theresa on the floor. I left the driver's seat and walked to the rear of the camper to get a look at the guy behind us.

Like his buddy, he was unshaven and had long dark hair. However, this guy was morbidly obese, a fact that was obvious even with most of his body hidden from view. I couldn't make a weight estimate, but he was clearly enormous.

He stared at me, looking almost bored.

"I think Roger and I should go out there and talk to them."

"Andrew, no!" said Helen.

"Maybe they're just playing a joke. Seeing how long we'll sit in here. I mean, what else could they possibly be doing? They're not attacking us or trying to steal our camper or anything like that."

"Maybe they're waiting for somebody else."

And then the guy behind us began to back up. He pulled back nearly ten feet then stopped.

"He's moving," I announced.

"The guy up here is saying something," Roger informed everybody. "Not to us, he must be talking into a walkie-talkie or something."

"It damn well better not be a cell phone," I muttered.

The truck in front of us honked. "Roger, switch places," I said, and we crossed paths in the middle of the camper as I returned to the driver's seat.

The truck honked again.

I honked back and gave him the finger.

Goblin grinned. It was *not* a grin that left me with a warm fuzzy feeling inside.

I started up the engine. "I think he wants me to back up," I said. What I really wanted to do was floor the gas pedal and knock the grinning prick off the road, but even though our vehicle had the size advantage it would never work, at least not without wrecking the camper.

I slowly backed up. The truck moved forward to match my progress.

"The guy behind us is backing up, too," Roger told me.

We continued moving, blocked between the two trucks. Maneuvering around the first corner was tricky, but I did it without us going off the road.

"What do we have in the way of weapons?" Samantha asked from above.

"Not much," I said. "Unless somebody packed a machine gun without permission."

"Stay up here, honey," Samantha told Kyle, before jumping down. "I'll see what I can find. We've at least got the fishing poles if we get really desperate."

"They're packed at the bottom," said Helen.

Fishing poles. The weapon of choice for the traveler in distress.

We also had lots and lots of marshmallows. Maybe we could immobilize these guys with sticky gooey goodness.

It was a long, scary drive. Roger moved back up to the front while Samantha gave us reports from the rear. Helen and Theresa moved up to the top bunk with Kyle. Joe slept on the floor. The trucks maintained their close proximity to us, never giving me an opportunity to slam on the gas and speed ahead of the one in front, even if there'd been room to get past him.

"You know, we could've handled the Wreitzer Park earwigs just fine," Roger remarked, forcing a smile.

"I think we're almost back to the store," said Samantha. "Do either of you remember if there was a phone inside?"

I glanced at Roger. He shrugged. "We're not sure," I admitted.

"I can't imagine that there wouldn't be." Samantha looked through the open window on the left side of the camper. "When we get just a little bit closer, I'm gonna jump out and make a run for it."

"The hell you will," said Roger.

"We have no idea where they're taking us or what their plans are. What if they're just forcing us to some abandoned area to butcher us? This may be our only chance to get help."

"What if they have guns?"

"I've gotta risk it."

Roger took a deep breath, looking distressed. "You're right, we have to try something. But I'll do it."

Samantha shook her head. "I can run the fastest. Don't worry, I'll be okay. I promise."

"You should take my cell phone," said Helen. "Maybe it'll work outside the camper."

"No. If something happens to me, you'll need it."

"But nothing *is* going to happen to you."

Samantha considered that, and then took the cell phone. "Thanks."

I have to admit, sending our phone along with the woman who would soon be in serious danger didn't sound like a very good idea, but I didn't protest.

Samantha gave Roger a quick kiss then placed her hands on the window sill and prepared to leap out. "Andrew, when I tell you to, stop the camper just long enough for me to jump."

I felt sick to my stomach. Sure, I didn't like Samantha, but I certainly didn't want her to put her life at risk! Though she could technically make it into the woods in just a few strides, it would be at least another twenty or thirty feet before the trees became thick enough to hide her.

Roger looked as if he wanted to grab her arm and hold her back, but after a moment of indecision he went to the rear of the camper.

"Stop!" she said.

I applied the brake.

Samantha immediately leapt out of the camper.

Without hesitation, Goblin braked to a halt.

He reached down for something.

Samantha darted toward the woods.

"The one in back has a gun!" Roger cried out.

Goblin raised a gun of his own. A shotgun. He pointed it out of his passenger side window and quickly took aim.

Samantha hurried off the road.

I slammed my foot on the gas pedal.

The camper bashed into the truck, throwing me against the steering wheel. The shotgun fired, but the shot went wild.

Another gunshot went off behind the camper.

I put the camper into reverse.

"*Shit!*" Roger screamed.

I slammed the gas pedal again. The camper smashed into the truck behind us as a third gunshot fired.

"Did he hit her? What happened?" Helen demanded over Theresa and Kyle's screams. Joe ran from one end of the camper to the other, barking furiously.

"He got her!" Roger shouted. "Oh, *God!*"

I glanced out the window, catching a quick glimpse of motion in the woods and a blur of red. Then I looked at the truck in front of us and put the camper back into drive.

Goblin had his shotgun pointed at me.

I ducked down as he fired, shattering the front windshield. Safety glass sprayed all over me.

"Andrew, reverse!" Roger shouted.

Staying ducked down, I put the camper into reverse once more. Another shot fired from behind us, not quite as loud as the shotgun blasts. It was followed by two more before I could send the camper rocketing backward again. As we collided with the truck, I kept the gas pedal floored, trying to push that maniac right off the road.

More bullets fired, slamming into the seat above my head.

The camper suddenly felt like it was going to topple. I let up on the gas and applied the brake.

"Is everybody okay?" I asked. I could hear Theresa and Kyle sobbing, but it didn't sound like either of them had been hurt. "Helen?"

"I'm fine," she said. "We're all fine in here."

"Roger?"

"I think she made it," he announced, sounding out of breath. "They shot her in the arm, I don't know how bad, but she got away!"

I put the camper into park. Joe pressed his flat face against my leg, whimpering.

Now what?

"That was really stupid," Goblin called out. "There's nobody out here who'll help her, and she'd bleed to death before she found them anyway!"

I hoped he wasn't just cleverly trying to psyche us out. The store owner could certainly be in on it...but for now I'd remain optimistic.

If Samantha *did* get in touch with the police, how long would we have to defend ourselves against these psychos before help arrived? We'd never even found the fishing poles.

I waited silently for a few moments. I couldn't hear any activity outside. Maybe they were conserving ammunition. Maybe their guns were empty. I wasn't about to pop my head into view to check it out.

Then I heard another vehicle approach from the rear.

"Is this bad?" I asked Roger.

"Real bad," he informed me. "Three more trucks."

Maybe they were coming in peace. Maybe they'd talk some sense into the other two, we'd all have a nice chuckle over this silly misunderstanding, and we'd get together for a late lunch and a friendly pillow fight.

Or maybe not.

"Forget this," I said. "We're getting out of here. I'll plow right over one of these trucks if I have to. Everybody hold on."

I floored the gas pedal.

And then I very quickly realized that this had been an extraordinarily bad idea, right in line with many of my other extraordinarily bad ideas of the past. The camper began to topple to the right.

As everybody else screamed and I held onto the steering wheel as tightly as I could, the camper fell onto its side with an almost deafening crash.

Chapter Six

I tumbled out of the driver's seat and smashed against the other side of the camper as glass rained down upon me. Joe landed on my side with a yelp.

How could I have been so stupid?

The answer was simple: It was me.

I could hear sobbing and screaming in the back of the camper, which was a hell of a lot better than corpse silence. "Everybody talk to me!" I called out.

"We're all alive," Helen said.

"You suck, Andrew!" Roger informed me.

I twisted myself around and got to my feet. On the other end of the overturned camper, the bathroom door was hanging open and swinging next to Roger as he tried to move past it.

I was sore and a little dizzy, but I crouched down and made my way back to the main part of the camper, walking on top of the refrigerator door. Helen was crawling out of what had been the upper bunk. She had a nasty gash on the side of her head but looked otherwise unharmed.

Helen grabbed Theresa's arms, and I grabbed Kyle's, and we quickly helped our children out of the bunk. I gave Kyle a tight hug, trying to forget for a moment that we were still very deeply screwed.

"What was that all about?" Goblin shouted. I heard a door slam, as if he'd gotten out of his truck. "Do you think this improved your situation?"

"Bite me!" I replied, proving my spirit wasn't yet broken but that I was too shaken up to think of anything more clever to say than "Bite me."

Then I thought, *oops, I should've shut up and pretended to be dead.* What a dork.

"We're not here to kill you," Goblin said, "but we'll do it if we have to, no problem."

"What's our other option?" I asked.

"Come out and give yourselves up."

That didn't sound like a very good option. On the other hand, if their master plan had been to just blow us all away, they wouldn't have bothered with the whole trap-us-between-two-trucks thing.

There had to be a way out of this. Quite honestly, I was more comfortable with the idea of sprinting toward the woods and dodging bullets than surrendering.

Joe barked.

"We'll even let the dog go," Goblin promised, and the others chuckled. They sounded close.

Unfortunately, with the camper on its side, our methods of escape were limited. Climbing up through the windows on top was a sure way to get a shotgun blast through the skull, leaving only the broken front windshield and the rear window. The rear window had shattered in the fall but so much of our camping junk was piled in front of it there wasn't room to climb out.

At least, no room for anybody but Joe. Yet somehow I didn't see this particular pug as one that would perform Lassie services for our family.

"Are you sure we can't settle this through a bribe?" I asked, silently ushering Helen and the kids toward the front windshield. "We've got marshmallows."

"Sorry. Ogre might go for it, but not the rest of us."

I wondered who Ogre was. Probably the huge guy in the second truck.

"What if we toast them first?" I asked.

"I'm not here to perform a fuckin' comedy routine with you," Goblin said. "You've got ten seconds to come out here before things get really ugly. Nine...eight...seven..."

"My wife's leg is broken!" I said. "She can't move."

"...six...five..."

"It's pinned under some suitcases! She can't go anywhere!" I moved over to the rear of the camper, where Roger was hurriedly moving our gear out of the way.

"...four...three...two..."

"I'm serious!"

"...one. Time's up. How about we toast those marshmallows for you?"

Seconds later, a bottle fell through the broken window on what was now the camper's ceiling. A bottle with burning cloth stuffed into the neck. The Molotov cocktail struck the wood paneling and burst into flames, separating me from my family and forcing Roger and I more tightly against the rear of the camper.

As the camper quickly filled with smoke, Joe rushed around the flames, barking loudly, over to where Roger and I stood. I could barely see Helen on the other side, her arms wrapped tightly around Theresa and Kyle.

A second Molotov cocktail fell right where the first had landed.

I'd been in worse situations in my life, but this sucked pretty intensely.

I picked up the closest weapon: Kyle's Wiffle bat.

Roger found one of the fishing poles.

A third Molotov cocktail shattered against the wood, which kind of seemed like overkill by this point. The camper was now so filled with smoke I couldn't see my wife and kids anymore, though I heard Helen coughing.

Joe squirmed underneath a blanket.

Obviously, we couldn't stay in the camper any longer. I crawled out through the rear window, coughing as well. Though my eyes burned and my vision was a bit blurry, the shotgun barrel two feet from my face was perfectly clear.

Roger followed me. He immediately was faced with a shotgun barrel of his very own.

A woman held the shotgun pointed at me. She had dirty black hair cut short, and looked about forty. Her blue jeans had holes in the knees and she wore a white lab coat with a few dried bloodstains. Her ID badge identified her as "Witch."

Roger's new buddy, "Troll," was also in his forties. He wore shorts and a light blue t-shirt, which showed off dozens, maybe hundreds, of scars on his arms and legs. There were also four or five fresh cuts. A large knife with a serrated edge dangled from his belt, and he wore a rather nice tie that matched his shirt.

Smoke billowed from the overturned camper, and I couldn't see Helen, Kyle, and Theresa behind it.

"Look at this mess you made," said Goblin, gesturing toward the camper and damaged trucks as he walked over to us. "That was pretty damn stupid. I should have Troll cut you up for that."

Troll flashed me a rotten-toothed grin.

Helen stepped into view from behind the camper, staggering a bit. She held Kyle and Theresa's hands. The big guy (five hundred pounds, at least) I assumed was Ogre was behind them, along with a kid who looked about twenty.

"Oh, yeah, he could cut you up *real* nice," said Goblin. "Make you look as bad as he does. Do you have a special attachment to any of those fingers of yours? How about your nose?" He flicked my nose with his index finger. "Would you mind so terribly if he sliced off your nose?"

I didn't respond.

"What about the kids' noses? Would you like that?" He looked over at Theresa and Kyle, and then back at me. "They're yours, right? They kind of look like you. Let's just hope they grow up with better problem-solving skills than you."

Goblin didn't seem particularly worried about any other vehicles approaching, so clearly they'd blocked off the road. He also didn't seem concerned about Samantha's escape, which probably wasn't a good sign.

"Don't you have anything clever to say?" Goblin asked me. "You were pretty clever in the camper. You made the marshmallow comment, remember? Joking in the face of danger. Pretty brave. Say something clever now."

"A husband and wife were both fortunetellers who desperately needed money, so they decided to have a kid. Do you know why?"

Goblin frowned. "Why?"

"To make a little prophet."

Goblin just stared at me.

"I made that up," I said.

"Just now?"

"No. But I thought it was pretty clever. Your turn."

Goblin smiled. "Sure. Troll, do me a favor and slice off his hand. Is that clever enough for you?"

Troll handed his shotgun to Goblin, keeping it pointed at me, then withdrew the knife from his belt.

Then Joe ran out of the camper, still covered in the blanket. It was, in fact, Kyle's blanket, featuring the children's television abomination *Zany the Chipper Chipmunk*. The poor dog ran in circles, desperately trying to get untangled.

Goblin and the others watched with amusement.

"Don't hurt Joe!" Kyle wailed.

"Don't hurt Joe?" Goblin asked. "How about I put Joe out of his misery?"

Out of the corner of my eye, I saw Helen move. She kicked Ogre exactly where I'm sure he least wanted to be kicked, where he had no blubber to protect him, and she kicked *hard*. The behemoth dropped to his knees and howled in agony.

In a flash, Helen, Theresa, and Kyle fled toward the woods, followed by the kid.

I swung the Wiffle bat as hard as I could, smacking Witch on the side of the head. You'd be amazed what kind of impact you can get with one of those things. Though Witch didn't drop her shotgun, she definitely felt some pain.

Roger smacked Troll with the fishing pole, which snapped in half.

Goblin spun around and aimed the shotgun at Helen.

Fired.

As I lunged at him, he spun the shotgun back at me, catching me in the face with the barrel. I fell to the ground.

Troll stabbed at Roger with the knife, missing by millimeters.

Goblin pressed the barrel of the shotgun against my chest.

I glanced over and watched as Ogre got to his feet and hurried off into the woods with surprising speed for somebody so large. I couldn't see Helen, but I could hear her shouting for Theresa and Kyle to run faster, shouting with far too much energy for her to have been shot.

Goblin pushed down hard on the shotgun, grinding the hot barrel into my chest. I let out an involuntary yelp of pain.

Something happened to Roger. I didn't see what. He fell to the ground next to me.

A gunshot fired in the woods.

Then another.

"What do you think? I bet that second one went through your daughter's fucking skull!" Goblin sneered, raised the shotgun barrel just a bit, and then slammed it back down onto my chest. "Maybe the first one only wounded your wife. Maybe she'll bleed to death. Sound good to you?"

Another gunshot.

"Oooooh, I bet that one got your son. His brains are probably splattered all over one of those trees. Wanna go see?"

Witch laughed and kicked Roger in the side.

An agonized scream sounded from the woods.

Joe, finally free of the blanket, hurried after Helen and the kids.

Goblin frowned. "Was that Ogre?"

Witch nodded. "Sounded like him."

"Troll, go see what's going on."

Another agonized scream, but not one of physical pain.

Troll rushed toward the woods, then stopped as Ogre emerged from behind the burning camper, holding the kid in his arms. The kid was limp, his shirt soaked with blood. "She got Ghoul!" Ogre screamed. "The bitch shot him!"

Goblin turned away from me but kept the shotgun in place. "Oh, Christ, no. How bad is he hurt?"

Ogre was almost in tears. "I dunno...I think he's dying...she got him really bad..."

"Cover them," Goblin said to Witch as he hurried over to the others. "Hey, Ghoul, can you hear me? You can hear me, right? You're gonna be okay, I promise!"

Ogre crouched down and gently set the kid down on the ground. Goblin pulled up his shirt to examine the wound. "Aw, shit! *Shit!*" He ran his hand through Ghoul's hair. "It's fine, you'll be fine, we'll get you help."

Witch looked like she desperately wanted to go over and help out, but she kept her shotgun pointed at Roger and me.

"Get me something to stop the bleeding!" Goblin gestured frantically. "There! Get that blanket the dog was in!"

Troll grabbed Kyle's blanket and tossed it over to Goblin. Goblin pressed the corner of the blanket against Ghoul's chest. I couldn't see Ghoul's face, but he certainly didn't seem to be moving.

Goblin kept one hand pressed against the blanket and wiped his eyes with the other. "What the hell is the matter with us today? We lost four of 'em, Ghoul got shot...this is bullshit!"

Ogre glared at me. "We'll make those two suffer."

"Oh yeah," said Goblin. "We'll chop them up. We'll cut them down to the *molecular* level. Troll, go after the wife and kids. But be careful, it sounds like she has a gun."

Troll shook his head. "I'm staying with Ghoul."

"I didn't say it was optional!"

"I'll get them," said Ogre. "I'll rip her head off. She won't get very far with two little kids."

"Fine, you go then. But hurry!"

Ogre ran off into the woods.

"How's he doing?" Witch asked.

"He's coughing up blood...I don't think he's going to..." Goblin trailed off. "Aw, Christ."

"What?"

"I think he's dead. Yeah, he is. He's gone."

"Are you sure?"

"I'm sure."

Witch cursed under her breath as her eyes glistened.

I kicked her in the shin as hard as I possibly could and grabbed the barrel of the shotgun. Roger jumped up and lunged for the weapon as well, quickly wrenching it out of her grip. Before Goblin could open fire, Roger had the shotgun jammed against Witch's back.

"Drop your gun or you'll lose another one!" Roger shouted as Goblin pointed the shotgun at me.

"Just blow him away!" Witch demanded.

Goblin hesitated.

We stood in silence for a long moment. I couldn't help but cringe, expecting Goblin to pull the trigger at any instant.

Finally Goblin chuckled without humor. "This has been one unproductive day."

"Drop the shotgun or I'll kill her!" Roger shouted. "I mean it!"

"Really?" asked Goblin. "You're the kind of guy who would shoot a woman in the back, huh?"

"If I have to, yeah."

"And what if I call your bluff?"

"Then we might have another four dead bodies here."

Goblin considered that. "So you're saying you and I would end up killing each other at the same time, right?"

"That's right."

"Seems unlikely. I think the more realistic scenario is three dead bodies, not four."

"Maybe. But if I shoot you before you shoot me, I'll take out your friend back there, too. That's four."

"But you only have two shells."

On one hand, I wanted to call for an end to this ridiculous conversation, but on the other hand, it was keeping me alive.

"One last time," said Roger. "Drop the gun."

Goblin shook his head. "I'm not going to drop the gun. You know that. I'm fully prepared to take this as far as it will go."

"So am I."

"Then there's a lot more blood to come. But let me make a counter-offer. Let Witch go and I'll let you go. I don't care how we do it...you guys can slowly back into the woods and keep your gun pointed at her, it doesn't matter to me, but you might want to speed it up a bit, because I'll wager Ogre isn't too far behind your friend's wife and kids if he hasn't caught them already."

Roger glanced at me. I nodded. Sure, I didn't trust these guys, but I definitely wasn't in favor of a shotgun blast to the stomach.

Roger backed up a couple of steps, keeping the gun pointed at Witch. I backed up as well. The others watched us carefully.

We backed up a few more steps, more quickly now.

It really did look like they were going to let us go.

And then the damn camper exploded.

Chapter Seven

A piece of shrapnel, I'm not sure exactly what, slashed across my cheek as Roger and I were thrown to the ground by the force of the blast. I struck the dirt hard and my shoulder instantly went numb.

Roger's shotgun fell out of his hands and went off, putting a huge bloody hole in the side of one of the lunatics. Unfortunately, that lunatic was Ghoul, who was already conveniently dead.

Goblin, Witch, and Troll hit the ground as well, but they were recovering quickly. As we all started to get back up, it was clear our best bet was to rely upon the age-old tradition of getting the hell out of there as fast as we could.

There were only two options: Run into the left side of the woods, following Samantha, or run into the right side of the woods, following Helen and the kids.

Since we were already on the left side of the road, going after Helen would've added a few more seconds to our dash, almost guaranteeing we'd be shot down.

Roger ran to the left.

I followed him.

We made it into the woods right before the first shot went off, striking a tree just inches from my head. Several more shots fired as we sprinted amongst the trees, emitting obscenities at an almost supernatural rate.

I knew we'd have to circle around and go after my family, but for now our only chance to stay alive was to run.

Though the gunshots continued, nobody seemed to be pursuing us.

After about a minute, they stopped shooting.

After about five minutes, we stopped running.

"Are you sure it's safe?" asked Roger, as I slowed down to a walk.

I shook my head. "It's probably not. But we can't afford to get lost, not with everybody else still out there."

Roger suddenly looked crestfallen. "Do you think Samantha's okay?"

"She's probably riding a tank to our rescue right now."

"I'm sure Helen got away," Roger assured me. "And, hell, if they *did* catch her, you know they'd regret it in a big way."

I smiled, although it was more than a little forced. "Yeah, all she'd have to do is give them The Gaze and they'd run screaming like babies."

"Absolutely."

We walked in silence for a moment. I ran my finger across the cut on my cheek and found it wasn't bleeding too badly. At least I had that going for me.

"Oh, and I paid extra for insurance on the camper," I finally said. "Good call, huh?"

"You're the man."

"This is the new Andrew Mayhem. Yeah, I'm still spending half of my life pursued by homicidal deviants, but I'm doing it knowing the damages to the camper are fully covered."

"I always knew you had it in you to become a responsible citizen."

I sighed. This joking around really wasn't helping me feel any less terrified about what might be happening to my wife and children.

"Maybe we should call out for Samantha," Roger said.

"That'll give away our position."

"Yeah, but I don't think they chased us. She might need help."

I nodded. "You're right."

Roger cupped his hands around his mouth and shouted Samantha's name.

Silence.

And then, distantly: "I'm here!"

She was to our left, in the direction of the store. Roger immediately took off running and we sprinted toward the sound of her voice.

She called out once more as we ran, and it took three or four minutes to reach her. Or at least where we thought she was.

"Samantha?" Roger called out.

"I'm here!" she said, sounding extremely close. "Down here!"

Down here? That didn't sound good.

And it wasn't.

Samantha had fallen into a pit, about six feet square and six feet deep. She was pinned against the side, her hair messed up, her face contorted with pain, and her shoulder covered with blood.

Her arms were fully extended and her hands were pressed tightly against a large vertical wooden board, the same size as the pit and about two inches thick. Dozens of wooden spikes were imbedded in it. From the gash on Samantha's right hand, it looked like one of the spikes had ripped across her index finger as she blocked the board.

The board was on a giant spring that protruded from the site of the pit. Clearly, when she'd fallen into the pit, the spring had released, hurtling the board at her. A bunch of dirt and some crumpled cellophane showed how they'd hidden the trap.

Roger crouched down next to the edge of the pit. "How long have you been holding that thing?"

"I'm not sure...a few minutes..."

"Just keep holding on. We'll get you out of there."

"I don't know if you can," said Samantha, her voice trembling. "I'm only still alive because my foot got wedged under it."

I glanced down. Indeed, her right foot was extended and stuck underneath the board. It looked excruciatingly painful.

"How bad is it?" Roger asked.

"Broken, for sure. I might be able to pull it out, but if I do, I won't be able to hold this thing back."

"Don't worry, you'll be fine," Roger insisted. "It really doesn't look all that bad from up here."

Some sweat trickled into Samantha's eyes and she blinked it away. "You're cute when you lie."

I grabbed a branch off the ground, broke it in half, and tried to wedge it between the wall of the pit and the board. It was too long to fit. I broke off a piece of it, tried again, and it dropped to the bottom. This is why I failed shop class in high school.

Roger placed his hands against the top of the board and tried to push. "I can't get any leverage."

There was no way sticks were going to work. I leapt down into the safe side of the pit, gripped the top of the board, and tried to pull it back. It refused to budge. Roger jumped down and helped me, and with the two of us working together, pulling as hard as we could, we managed to move it just a bit...

But just a bit is all. And what would happen when Samantha got her foot free?

"Guys, I can't feel my arms, I'm not sure how much longer I can hold this."

Roger let go of the board. "Pulling isn't working. We'll have to push."

I'd really hoped he wasn't going to suggest that. We quickly climbed out of the pit and moved back to Samantha's side. Though her face was firm with resolve, her arms were shaking. Her breath began to come in quick gasps.

"Roger, I love you..."

Roger swung his legs over the side of the pit.

"What are you doing?" Samantha demanded.

"I've never had the chance to experience a good old-fashioned spiked pit," said Roger, leaping down all the way and bracing his arms against the board. "Andrew, get me stuff to wedge against the bottom."

I gathered up several branches and dropped them down into the pit. Roger kicked the cellophane away and used his foot to try and shove them underneath the board as best he could.

It didn't look like anything was going to hold.

Roger looked up at me, his face already covered with perspiration. "When she gets her foot free, pull her out of here."

Samantha gave a couple of hard tugs. "It's not coming loose." She tugged several more times in rapid succession, gasping in pain with each one. "Roger, get out of here! I mean it!"

"You can do it," Roger insisted. "Keep trying!"

"It's not coming free! Damn it, Roger, you're going to die!"

I can't believe I'm going to do this, I thought.

"If I get poked by so much as one solitary spike, I'm kicking both of your asses," I said, dropping into the pit.

I crouched down, accidentally scraping my face against one of the spikes. It was the same side that had been cut by the shrapnel from the exploding camper. Nice.

I reached down and grabbed hold of Samantha's lower leg with both hands, trying to ignore the spike that was ready to fly right through my eye, then pulled back as hard as I could.

Her foot popped free.

The board moved back an inch. While none of them broke the skin, spikes were now poking me in at least four places. To keep a sunny outlook on things, I noted that none of those places were my eye. I stood back up and pressed my hands against the board.

"My, this was a *splendid* idea," I proclaimed, using my foot to try and wedge more branches underneath the board. "Wouldn't it be hilarious if the bad guys showed up right about now?"

There was virtually no room to maneuver, but I managed to turn myself around with only a few nasty scrapes, and then pulled myself out of the pit.

"Give me your hands," I told Samantha.

"Go ahead," said Roger. "I've got it." He didn't sound convinced.

Samantha hesitantly lifted her hands. Roger let out a loud grunt at the additional strain but managed to keep the spikes out of his body. I grabbed Samantha's wrists and pulled her out of the pit.

His girlfriend was safe, but Roger was still in a bit of a pickle.

"These branches aren't going to hold it," Roger said, voice cracking.

I quickly sat down on the edge of the pit. "Maybe we can hold it with our legs." I braced my feet against the board and then tightly gripped the edge of the pit with my hands to hold myself in place.

"Have you got it?" Samantha asked.

"I think so."

"I'll help." She sat down on the other side of Roger and placed both of her feet against the board. Her right shoe was completely red.

"Roger, on the count of three, let go and get out of there," I said. "One...two...three!"

Roger let go of the board and turned around.

I felt my knees begin to bend.

Samantha let out an agonized whimper.

Roger spun around and tried to scramble out of the pit.

My grip was beginning to loosen.

Roger was halfway out.

"Hurry up!" I said, as if he'd been lollygagging.

Just as Roger got his legs safely out of the way, I lost my grip. The board hurtled forward, pushing Samantha and I off balance, and slammed into the wall of the pit.

"Whoa!" Roger shouted.

"Whoa," I said in agreement.

Tears were streaming down Samantha's face. I couldn't imagine how badly her foot must hurt. Even hellspawn feel pain. "Are you okay?" Roger asked, putting his arms around her.

She nodded, and then turned her head and spit out some blood. "I bit my tongue trying not to scream."

I stood up, still breathing heavily. "Is there any chance that you can walk?"

"No, but I can hop with the best of them." She suddenly looked horrified. "Helen and the kids! Where are they? Are they okay?"

"I don't know. I...I'm sure they are, but I don't know. I need to go on ahead in case they're already at the store. Were you able to call the police?"

Samantha shook her head. "I dropped the phone when I got shot. I'm sorry."

"Crap." I should have protested when Helen offered to give her the phone. Of course, I also should have avoided tipping the camper on its side. "Well, I'm going on ahead. You two stay here, out of sight." I quickly stripped out of my shirt and handed it to Roger. "Here, use this to help clean up her foot and shoulder."

"What, you're not donating your jeans, too?"

"You're lucky you got the smelly shirt."

"Thanks, Andrew," said Samantha. "You'll find Helen and the kids, I promise."

"Be careful out there," Roger told me. "I've heard rumors that there are spiked pits in these woods."

I nodded and ran off in the direction of the store.

Chapter Eight

I watched the ground carefully as I ran, which caused me to smack into no fewer than three different branches. Fortunately, though, I didn't fall into any spiked pits, get caught in any bear traps, get struck by any poisoned darts, or bash into the gates of Hell.

Finally the woods thinned and I emerged next to the store. There were still no cars in the parking lot.

I cracked my knuckles nervously. Hopefully Helen and the kids were inside. And hopefully the old guy in there wasn't involved with this whole mess. I had several dozen other "hopefully"'s I could think of, including one about machine guns and expensive armor dropping from the sky, but I decided to stick with those two for the time being.

I considered going around back to find a way to sneak in, but I'd already wasted too much time at the pit-o-spikes. I'd just have to be really, really careful.

I walked over to the front door, took a deep breath, then opened it and stepped inside.

No hailstorm of bullets ripped my chest apart, which was a promising beginning. The old man still sat behind the counter, reading his magazine. He looked a bit startled to see me.

"Forget something?" he asked. "Like maybe your shirt?"

"Do you have a phone?"

He shook his head. "No need for one."

"No need for one? How can you run a place of business without a phone?"

"Got a wireless modem on my PC in the back room. I can use the Internet to place all of my orders quickly and efficiently."

"Ah. Has anybody else been here since me?"

"Since now or since the first time you were here?"

"The first time."

"Nope."

"Can I borrow your computer for a minute? It's an emergency."

"Nope. It's a fancy piece of equipment and it's not for customer use. You'll be downloading that damn pornography and getting my machine all filled with viruses and I'm not gonna let it happen."

"No, I just need to contact the police."

The old man chuckled. "You went to Wreitzer Park anyway, didn't you? I told you—"

"No, we were taking your advice but we got ambushed. These people in trucks blocked our way and the camper tipped over and I got separated from my wife and kids and I desperately need to use your computer."

The old man stroked his chin thoughtfully. "You sure are anxious to look at pornography."

"I'm not interested in pornography! My family is in danger!"

"Now, I'm not saying I don't enjoy a good nudie magazine every now and then, if the breasts are natural," the old man informed me. "I just don't want any of that stuff on my computer."

I gaped at him for a moment. He was definitely part of this whole mess. That was their *modus operandi*, to be as annoying as humanly possible.

I wasn't in the habit of beating information out of old men (I usually just tied them up and threatened them with broken plates), but perhaps I could give it a shot just this once.

A vehicle pulled up outside.

The old man looked me in the eye. "I'm not the kind of fellow to tell somebody their business, but you may want to hide."

I quickly moved away from the counter and ducked into the aisle at the far end of the store. I pushed a box of cereal out of the way, allowing me to peek through the shelf and watch the front counter.

Now I was getting more than a bit confused. So, was the old man aware of what was going on, but he was actually a good guy? Or maybe he genuinely *was* concerned I might use his computer to access pornographic images or videos.

I looked around for something to use as a weapon. As in the camper, my options were limited, although the cat food, hurled in sufficient quantities, looked like it could do some damage.

The door opened.

"Hey, Charlie, how's it going?" asked a voice I was pretty sure belonged to Troll. As he walked up to the front counter I saw it was indeed Troll, he of the scarred legs.

"It's going fine. How've you been?" asked the old man. "I haven't seen you around here since you shoplifted this morning."

Troll sighed. "It's going like complete shit, Charlie. We lost Ghoul."

"Better get out there and find him."

"We didn't *lose* him lose him, dumb-ass. He's dead."

"Are you kidding?"

I considered moving down to the other end of the aisle so I could make a break for it, but if I was lucky, Troll and Charlie wouldn't waste too much time talking and I'd get my chance to contact the police.

Troll shook his head. "Completely serious. He could be a pain sometimes, but I really liked that kid, and it's never good to lose a member of your team, y'know?"

"It certainly isn't."

Troll withdrew his hunting knife from its leather sheath. "And to top it all off, every one of 'em got away. I mean, even the frickin' *dog*. I'll tell you something, Charlie, I think this team is falling apart."

Troll began to scrape the knife against his leg. It appeared to be an absent-minded action, but I couldn't be sure.

"Well, you'll get them," said Charlie. "You always do. That's what the traps are for, right?"

"No, the traps are to give me something fun to do in between hunting sessions so I don't get bored out of my mind sitting around this dump. The specimens aren't even supposed to make it out of the car until we're ready. But yeah, they're probably dead. Hopefully chopped in half. I just think maybe we need new management, if you know what I mean."

"Yep, I know what you mean."

"So have you seen anybody in here since you reported the family?"

"Not a soul."

"If you do, let us know ASAP."

"Will do."

Troll slid the blade of the knife against the back of his leg. The cut wasn't deep, but a trickle of blood ran down his skin. He let out a soft moan of pleasure.

"What was that for?" asked Charlie.

"What?"

"That sound you made."

"It was nothing."

"Aw, jeez, Troll, are you cutting yourself again? Don't do that in my place. I'm not saying this is a respectable establishment, but I at least don't want that masochistic crap going on here. Cut yourself someplace else."

"Lighten up. I'm not gonna get any blood on your precious floor."

"I can mop the floor. I just don't want your nasty self-mutilation bullshit happening in my place of business. Knock it off."

Troll defiantly held up his left arm and very slowly slid the blade across it. He chuckled as Charlie grimaced.

"Get the hell out of my store," Charlie said, waving him away. "Come back when you learn to stop acting like a messed-up freak of nature."

"Got a Band-Aid?"

"Go on, get out of here, you whack-job. Go mourn your buddy."

I pulled back quickly as Troll looked over his shoulder in my direction. "Can I kill your guest first?"

"Aw, no, no, no!" Charlie protested. "Don't mess up my place!"

I stood up. My instinct was to run, but I'd be much better off if I stood and fought this particular whack-job, especially since Helen and the kids were probably heading this way. If I could get rid of Troll now, we'd be much more likely to ride off into the sunset for our happy ending.

I walked backwards as Troll joined me in the narrow aisle, grinning and holding the knife out in front of him. "Hey there. How've you been?"

"No, Troll, no! I mean it!" Charlie shouted. "No splatter on the merchandise! No splatter on the merchandise! That's the deal!"

"You really should adhere to your agreement," I suggested. "Getting banned from a store like this is a blot on your permanent record that will haunt you for the rest of your life."

"Oooooh, funny guy," said Troll.

"Really? I thought that joke was kind of lame. You must be easily amused."

"Oooooh, funny dead guy." Troll switched the knife from his right hand to his left. "Want me to carve some smiley faces on your chest?"

"No, but speaking of carving, what's the deal with cutting yourself? I mean, did you, I dunno, have a sexy French maid who cut you as punishment when you were a kid and it became some kind of fetish?"

Troll shrugged. "It's just my thing."

"It's a dumb thing. Really, it is. You look stupid when you're doing it. Chicks love scars, but not when they're self-imposed. I mean, I'm all for freedom of expression and all that, but what you're doing just isn't cool."

"Are you finished trying to distract me?"

"Almost."

Troll flicked the tip of his knife against his chin, drawing blood. "Maybe you should give this a try. You might like it."

"Nah, I've never been into that. I've always been a bludgeoning man, myself. So, do you use antiseptic in bulk, or is infection part of the whole allure?"

"Do you ever stop talking?"

"Not generally, no. How about this? You look like a pretty tough guy. Why not put down the knife and make this into a fair fight?"

"Why the hell would I want to do that?"

"To be honest, I have no idea. I'm just reaching at this point."

Then, without warning, he rushed at me. I instinctively grabbed for the closest object available, a bag of sour cream and onion potato chips, and used it to deflect his knife. The blade tore through the bag, releasing a shower of chips.

I punched him in the face as hard as I could. Troll flew back against the shelf, knocking several canned goods to the floor. He put a hand to his face where I'd punched him, smiled, and began to breathe heavily, almost panting.

Panting in a sexual way.

I truly hoped he didn't *enjoy* the punch.

He lunged at me with the knife again, and I stepped out of the way, crunching some chips underneath my foot. I punched him again, slamming my fist into his shoulder, and he let out a groan of pleasure.

"Not in here!" Charlie shouted, stepping into the aisle. "Some of us have to make a living!"

Troll rubbed his shoulder, pursed his lips, and said (and I quote): "Ooooooooh."

I lowered my fists. "Okay, no offense, but this is *seriously* messed up."

Troll grinned. "C'mon, give it to me again, big boy."

I grabbed a large can of tomato soup from the shelf and swung it at him just as he swung his knife at me. Tin can met stainless steel blade, and both lost. The can fell out of my hand and the knife fell out of his.

I punched him in the face with my other hand, knocking him back a step. He didn't throw back his head and scream "Yes! Oh, *yes!*" but his expression implied he was thinking it.

"You're paying for the damage, Troll! I'm gonna take inventory of every cent!"

"Shut up!" Troll shouted at him. "You're ruining this!"

This was so very wrong. How could I be expected to fight under these conditions?

Troll threw a punch of his own. It hit me in the chest, a glancing blow that was not even remotely pleasurable. Instead of punching back, I slammed my hands into his shoulders and gave him a hard push, shoving him to the floor. He landed on cans and potato chips, and this time his reaction was more of pain than pleasure, which was a relief.

I snatched up the knife.

Troll sat up and used the tip of his tongue to lick some of the blood trickling down the side of his mouth.

I held up the knife in what I hoped was a terribly intimidating way. "If you want to live, contact your buddies and tell them to call off the hunt."

"Why would I want to do that?"

"Because I just told you to. I don't think having this knife go through your eyeball will quite give you that happy-happy feeling."

"Couldn't tell you. I've never tried it." Troll slowly got back up, brushing potato chip fragments off his pants. "Hey, I've got an idea. Why don't you put that knife down so we can have a fair fight?"

"Okay," I said, flinging it at him.

I've never had much knife-throwing practice, but I hoped the blade would strike his throat, heart, or eyeball. It didn't. It struck his upper arm. He stared at the blade as it jutted out of his flesh, buried an inch deep.

He gasped.

Then gasped again.

Then let out a high pitched squeal of delight that was the single most disturbing noise I have ever heard in my entire life, and in the past couple of years of my life I've heard some really disturbing noises.

I rushed at him and punched at the knife, bashing it with my fist and jamming it even further into Troll's arm. He closed his eyes and sucked in a deep breath. A horrified glance downward revealed a bulge in his pants that was even more disturbing than the squeal.

"What the hell is the matter with you?" I demanded. "You're...you're...you're...you're wrong! You're just wrong!"

I wrenched the knife out of his arm and smashed the handle into his face. Troll hit the floor again, his head striking the large can of tomato soup. He let out a soft groan and then was still.

"Wrong!" I repeated.

I wiped my hands off on my shirt. My whole body felt icky.

I realized Charlie was still standing in the aisle, watching me. His eyes widened and he hurried away as I took off after him.

Chapter Nine

Catching Charlie wasn't difficult. I grabbed him by the back of the collar just as he reached the front counter and yanked him to the ground.

"It wasn't my fault!" he insisted. "I tried to keep him from hurting you!"

"No, you tried to keep him from sullying your merchandise with my blood. Tell me, were you lying about the phone?"

"No, I swear!"

"Were you lying about the computer?"

"Yes, I swear!"

"How were you going to contact Troll?"

"A walkie-talkie. It's behind the front counter. But I wasn't really going to contact him."

I dragged Charlie with me behind the counter. The two most notable things underneath the counter were a huge stack of porno magazines and a walkie-talkie. I grabbed the walkie-talkie but refrained from commenting on the magazines.

Charlie coughed. "Don't kill me. I wasn't going to rat on you, I swear. I hate helping these people, but they forced me to do it and they don't pay me much!"

The walkie-talkie had a hell of a lot more knobs and buttons on it than any walkie-talkie I'd ever used as a kid. "How does this work?" I asked.

"Press the big black button on the side."

I pressed the button. "Hello?" I said into the receiver.

A moment of silence, and then: "Troll?"

"No, this is Troll's captor. You may remember me from the exploding camper incident. To whom might I be speaking?"

"It's Goblin."

"Hi, Goblin. Look, I want to cut a deal. You let my wife and kids go, and I'll let your friend here go."

"How do I know you've really got him?"

I gestured at Charlie with the walkie-talkie. Charlie leaned into it and spoke. "It's me. Troll is unconscious on my floor."

I thought I heard a soft curse on the other end.

"I've already lost two of my closest friends," I said, hoping that if he thought Roger and Samantha were dead they wouldn't look for them, "and you've lost one. Now, we can keep whittling down each other's numbers, or we can cut our losses and call it quits right now."

"What do you mean, you lost two?"

"Exactly what I said. Call off the hunt and let us work out some kind of truce, or I'll slit Troll's throat with his own knife."

"Well, you see...who am I talking to, anyway?"

"Andrew."

"Well, Andrew, you see, we've got a bit of a problem here, because Ogre tends to have a lack of respect for my title, and he always got along really well with the boy your wife killed, so it seems unlikely he'd listen to me even if I did ask him to give up the chase."

"I'm not screwing around here," I said. "I'll kill him."

"I wasn't accusing you of screwing around. But, Andrew, another problem we've got is that Troll was never one of the more popular associates in our little group. I don't want to disrespect the poor guy when he's this close to death, but he actually made the rest of us kind of uncomfortable. Did you see that knife thing he does?"

"Yeah. What's up with that?"

"No idea." Goblin sighed on the other end. "You do what you've got to do, Andrew. I can't honestly say I want you to cut his throat, but I'm afraid it's not possible for us to work out a deal. I would like to leave you with one last thought, though: Now we know exactly where you are."

The door opened.

I spun around to see who it was, and caught a flash of Troll running out of the store.

Damn!

Before I'd even finished thinking the word "Damn," I heard another vehicle approach.

"Is there a back way out of here?" I asked Charlie.

He nodded.

I didn't think the old man would make a very good hostage. Most likely, they'd happily blow a hole right through his chest if I were standing behind him.

Keeping the walkie-talkie and the hunting knife with me, I rushed into the back room. It was filled with approximately eighty-seven tons of raw clutter and no computer. I spent a few seconds looking for a weapon but had no luck, so I threw open the door and ran outside, shutting the door behind me.

I'd made it about a hundred yards into the forest before I heard the door open again. I looked back and saw both Troll and Witch emerge. They immediately followed me, although Troll didn't seem to be quite as energetic as Witch.

I sprinted as quickly as I could. If I could get just far enough ahead that they couldn't see me, I'd try to loop around to the front of the store and steal one of their trucks.

Please don't trip, I told myself, since this seemed like the most appropriate moment for me to trip.

I didn't turn back but I could hear Witch's footsteps behind me. It sounded like she was gaining.

Then the footsteps stopped.

A gunshot fired, and several leaves flew into the air from the branch it struck. I'd thought I was running as fast as I could, but I picked up my pace nevertheless.

Another gunshot. This one seemed further off the mark, yet somehow I didn't feel like dancing a merry jig. My mind turned to other important matters, like the fact that I could fall into a spiked pit at any moment.

I glanced down, and promptly smacked into a branch.

Hard.

Though the branch didn't poke out anything, it was a violent enough blow that I found myself momentarily dazed. I stopped running and leaned my arm against the tree to keep my balance.

Just ahead I could see a tree much larger than the ones surrounding it. I'd hide behind it and pray they didn't find me. I stumbled over to the tree and cried out as a noose closed around my feet.

I was immediately yanked upside-down, causing me to drop the knife and walkie-talkie. I dangled there, about four feet off the ground, swaying back and forth.

Okay, this was pretty bad.

But it was important not to be cynical. After all, it was entirely possible that Troll and Witch might walk past without noticing the shirtless guy swinging upside-down from a tree. Or perhaps the blood rushing to my head might increase my powers of thought, allowing me to come up with an unbelievably creative solution to this whole problem involving tree sap, magnetic fields, and my own perspiration. Or I might look so pathetic hanging here that Troll and Witch would take pity on me and let me go.

If you really took the time to think about it carefully, getting caught in this trap was probably the best thing to happen to me all afternoon.

Definitely.

I heard Witch approach and moments later she stepped into view, smiling—as quite naturally she would since she wasn't the one hanging from a tree. Troll joined her, looking way too peppy for a guy who was still bleeding from being stabbed in the shoulder.

"Well, well, well," said Troll. "I'm glad to see my hard work setting up all of these traps paid off."

"Did you make all of them?" I asked.

"Yep."

"What's up with the spiked pit? Why take the time to set up that whole spring and board thing? If you'd put some spikes on the bottom it would've worked just as well."

"I have a lot of down time."

"Makes sense," I said, starting to get dizzy.

Witch took her walkie-talkie off her belt. "Goblin, you there?"

Goblin's voice crackled over the speaker. "Sure am."

"Troll and I have one of them. Do we kill him or bring him back?"

"Is it Andrew?"

Witch looked at me questioningly. I gave her an upside-down nod.

"Yeah," she said.

"Then definitely bring him back."

"You've got it. Witch out." She clipped the walkie-talkie back to her belt, and then turned to Troll. "I'll keep you covered. Get him down."

"Don't worry," Troll told me. "Pretty soon your body will be hurting a hell of a lot worse than your pride. Which is saying a lot."

He walked around the tree and out of sight. A moment later, I let out an embarrassing yelp and dropped to the ground, just barely managing to cushion my fall with my hands.

It was a close race, but yes, my body was indeed hurting worse than my pride. Of course, he probably wasn't referring to the fall, but rather fun stuff to come *after* the fall.

I pushed myself up. Maybe I could try the old throw-a-handful-of-dirt-into-the-bad-guy's-eyes-and-kick-them-in-the-stomach-while-they're-blinded trick.

Or maybe I could admit defeat.

"Look at me," said Witch.

I did.

"See this gun? We were told to take you back alive, but neither of us will be written up if that fails to happen. So if you try another stunt like you did back at the camper, or anything else, *anything*, I'll shoot you in the leg. If you try again, I'll empty the rest of this gun into your head. Do you understand me?"

I nodded.

"Say it."

"I understand."

"Good."

"Hey, looky here!" said Troll, wandering over and picking up his knife. "I've really missed this." He fondled it, flicked the tip against his leg, and then walked toward me. "Maybe I'll slice him up before we take him back. Just a little."

"Fine with me, if you do it quick," said Witch, keeping the gun pointed at my head.

I didn't even try to gather a handful of dirt. That would simply get me shot. As much as I hated to admit it, the only way I'd stay alive and possibly see my family again was to concede defeat.

For now.

Chapter Ten

Helen's Side

It's finally my turn.

My name is Helen Mayhem. I've been married to Andrew for a decade now, and I've had to put up with a lot. But you already knew that.

While I don't feel I've necessarily been misrepresented on these pages, give or take a few misquotes, I do think having only one point of view makes me appear quite a bit less sympathetic than I actually am. I'm not going to dwell on this, because I'm primarily referring to my husband's first two books and not this one, but I did want to suggest that if you've ever found me to be overly grouchy, demanding, and/or overbearing, that you stop to consider whether that attitude may have been justified.

The fact is, if you were married to Andrew, you'd think such an attitude was essential to your very survival.

I could probably go on for a couple of books of my own presenting my side of these adventures, but I don't want to interrupt the forward momentum any more than absolutely necessary. So I'll pick up where we left off, with me kicking Ogre in the testicles and fleeing into the woods.

I knew right away that simply running for our lives wasn't going to work, not with a seven and a nine-year-old in tow. We had to find a place to hide as quickly as possible. As we ran I looked for large overturned tree trunks, piles of branches, anyplace I could hide my children.

A shotgun fired. I'm not sure what it hit, but it wasn't me or my kids.

I grabbed Theresa and Kyle's hands and screamed for them to run faster. I could hear somebody following only steps behind us, so we ran with every ounce of energy we could muster.

He had to have a gun. All of them did, didn't they?

As far as I knew, we were only still alive at this moment because our pursuer had an aversion to shooting a woman and her children in the back.

The man behind us was gaining, and as close as he was he didn't have much more to gain. So I let go of my children's hands and came to a sudden stop, almost in the style of a Warner Brothers cartoon character.

I spun around and swung my fist. I didn't punch him so much as he ran into my fist with his jaw.

You know, it doesn't look that way on television, but it *hurts* to slam your fist into somebody's face. It hurts like you wouldn't believe. There's not a whole lot of cushioning in the jaw area, and I've got tiny little hands. For a second I almost thought my hand had popped off from the impact.

The man (not much more than a kid, actually) was knocked off his feet and his gun flew into the air.

I'd like to say I caught it in the dramatic fashion of an action movie star, but I didn't. It hit the ground next to him. I scooped it up.

The kid grabbed my arm.

I shot him in the chest.

I'd never killed anybody before. Never even injured anybody. Thus far in my life, I'd never delivered physical trauma more severe than a spanking, and I felt guilty for weeks over the spanking, even though Andrew deserved it.

Okay, I'm sorry, I shouldn't make a joke in the middle of this. I'm not as good at being witty as my husband, so I'm going to stick to a more or less straightforward telling of this narrative as much as possible. It's just that I feel somewhat compelled to use a lighthearted tone to help get me through this.

Because this time...well, things got really bad.

Blood splattered against my face.

I knew I'd have some hard times dealing with this later, but for now I was a pregnant woman defending her children and I was glad to shoot this son of a bitch.

His fingers tightened around my arm. I yanked away. His arm flopped to the ground.

Ogre, whose five hundred or so pounds had apparently recovered from the groin kick, came into view. He looked absolutely horrified.

I took a shot at him and missed.

I turned around. Kyle and Theresa were standing there, silent, almost in shock.

"Run!" I screamed at them, and then I quickly followed.

We raced through the woods. I prayed to God that Andrew was still alive, but I had to protect my children first.

Behind us, Ogre howled in grief.

We'd only been running for a couple of minutes before Kyle fell. I pulled him to his feet and tried to get him moving, but he fell again.

"Sweetheart, you have to get up," I insisted. "Do it for Mommy!"

Theresa looked back over her shoulder. "I hear Joe!"

I listened. I did in fact hear the dog barking. "Joe's going to be fine," I said. "We just have to keep running. Theresa, keep going!"

Theresa ran. I suddenly caught a reflection of light. My stomach gave a lurch, and I screamed: *"Theresa, stop!"*

She stopped.

I hurried over to her. There was a fishing line running between two trees, about six inches above the ground. I looked up in the tree and saw something metallic that was mostly hidden by the branches. I couldn't be sure what it was, but this whole thing definitely had the appearance of a booby trap.

I held out my hand and called Theresa back. "I'm going to hide you two, okay? I'm going to put you up in a tree where it's safe, and I'll be right here if anything happens, but I need you to be completely quiet, no matter what. Can you do that?"

"Yes, Mommy," said Theresa. Kyle nodded.

I watched the ground, now paranoid there might be traps lurking everywhere, and hurried over to a nice-sized tree with a low first branch. I hoisted Kyle up.

"Climb up a couple of branches and hide as much as you can. I'll let you know if I can see you or not."

As Kyle began to climb, I took Theresa to another tree about ten feet away and did the same.

I walked back and looked up into Kyle's tree. He was slightly visible, but only if you knew where to look. Once Theresa was equally well-hidden, I climbed a tree in the middle of the two and hid myself.

I didn't feel safe having myself and my kids trapped like this, with no way to escape, but I felt even less safe about running through booby-trapped wilderness.

Please let Andrew be okay, I thought.

And Roger.

And Samantha.

At least I knew Joe was doing okay. I could hear the dog barking as it ran.

What if Joe gave away our position?

"Kyle, Theresa, no matter what, do *not* say anything! Not a word! Not a noise!"

However, Joe's barking sounded pretty far away. He must've been going in the wrong direction. Not much of a tracker dog.

I was very proud of Theresa and Kyle. I couldn't hear any sign of them. I desperately hoped they'd get to meet their new little brother or sister.

I fidgeted with the gun in my hand. I wished I knew how many bullets I had left, but I wasn't exactly sure how to expel the clip and I didn't want to risk messing anything up.

I'd just have to make sure every shot counted.

We continued to wait. I wasn't wearing a watch, so I couldn't be sure how long we waited, but it was at least fifteen minutes and probably more.

Then I saw Ogre.

He was doing sort of a half-walk, half-run. He looked more insanely pissed than anybody I have ever seen, in real life or the movies. And he was coming our way.

How come the dog was off-course but the human was walking right toward us?

I carefully pointed the revolver at him. I didn't like the idea of being a sniper, but I could do it.

Mentally, that is. In terms of gun skills...well, I had none. I knew you pulled the trigger to fire and not much else. Yeah, I could shoot somebody in the chest when they were lying on the ground right in front of me, but beyond that my marksmanship skills were questionable.

I'd only shoot if absolutely necessary. The last thing I wanted to do was fire, miss, and discover I was out of bullets.

I held my breath as Ogre continued to move toward us.

Maybe we'd get lucky and he'd walk right through the booby trap. That would be nice.

I wished I'd climbed higher into the tree, but it was too late now.

He kept moving, belly jiggling with each step. His breathing was labored.

Then he slowed down, eyeing the trap. He gave the fishing line a wide berth, and then picked up his pace again, heading right for the gap between my tree and Kyle's.

He stopped right between them.

I hadn't heard a peep from Kyle. Maybe Ogre was just taking a break at an outrageously inconvenient location.

He looked up into the tree.

I stifled a whimper.

Ogre walked around to get a better look.

That was it. The big guy had to die. I pointed the gun at him and willed my arms to quit shaking so I could be absolutely, positively certain not to miss.

I held my aim steady. He was going to get it in the back of the head.

I squeezed the trigger.

The *click* sounded so loud that I was positive it had echoed throughout the entire forest.

Ogre spun around and looked for the source of the sound. Our eyes met, even though I was mostly hidden in the branches, and I knew he saw me.

Especially after he waved.

But though the gesture was lighthearted, Ogre looked no less furious.

I pulled the trigger several more times, hoping it had been a weapon malfunction and not that the gun was empty, but was rewarded with several more clicks.

While it seemed like a guy his size was unlikely to be up to the task of climbing trees, he could certainly call for reinforcements.

He removed the walkie-talkie from his belt and put it to his lips.

I leapt down from the tree.

He wasn't expecting this, but he still moved faster than I anticipated, and I landed feet-first on the ground instead of on his skull.

Then he punched me in the stomach so hard I thought his fist was going to rip through my back.

Mouth open, unable to catch a breath, I doubled over but somehow sustained my footing.

"*That* is for the kick to the crotch," Ogre told me. Then he clamped his enormous hand around my neck and lifted me back into a standing position. "This is for Ghoul."

He threw me into the air. I struck the ground and lay there, tasting blood, still unable to breathe, not sure if I'd ever be able to take a breath again.

"Where are your kiddies, Momma Bear?" Ogre asked, looking up in the trees. "It's been a while since breakfast, and I'm famished."

I tried to sit up, but I couldn't move. My body was paralyzed.

Ogre pointed up into Kyle's tree. "I see you, little boy! Do you want to know why they call me Ogre? Because I *eat* little boys just like you!"

I tried to scream for Kyle to climb higher, but I couldn't get my voice to work. I felt like I was going to suffocate right there.

"Why don't you come on down, little boy, and be my lunch? You know what the best part is? The nose. Yeah, I'll just bite your wee little nose right off."

I saw movement in the branches. Kyle was climbing.

"Oh, now, don't run away, little boy! It'll only make the fall hurt all that much worse."

With that, Ogre flung the walkie-talkie up into the tree. Kyle cried out and I saw the leaves flutter as he fell.

He grabbed onto the lowest branch and swung there, legs dangling.

With a powerful intake of breath, I sat up.

Kyle struggled mightily to pull himself up out of harm's way, but Ogre grabbed his leg.

"Leave him alone!" Theresa shrieked.

Kyle kicked Ogre in the face with his free foot. Ogre didn't even flinch.

He yanked my son free of the branch. Kyle fell into Ogre's arms, screaming in terror.

I got to my feet.

My vision was blurred, but it shot into sharp focus as Ogre opened his mouth, leaned his head down toward Kyle's upper arm, and took a bite.

Chapter Eleven

Helen's Side

The pain no longer mattered. Even hundred-pound metal chains wrapped around my entire body wouldn't have mattered. I was going to get my child away from that son of a bitch.

Kyle let out a wail that ripped through my heart. Ogre looked over at me and grinned a scarlet grin. A thick rope of blood and drool dangled from the corner of his mouth.

"Mmmmmmmmmm..." he said. "Nice and fresh."

I let out a howl of rage and rushed at him. I was going to tear him apart with my bare hands if I had to.

Ogre casually used his free hand to cuff me on the side of the head. I fell to the ground again.

"Mommy it hurts it hurts it *hurts*!" Kyle screamed. He began kicking violently, repeatedly slamming his feet into Ogre's gut, but the behemoth didn't even seem to feel it.

"I'm gonna grind your bones to make my bread," Ogre informed Kyle.

I got back up.

"Ooooh, Momma Bear's still got some fight left in her. She must love you a lot, little boy. Or maybe she wants to eat you herself, what about that?"

"Put him down!" I shouted.

Ogre licked the bloody wound on Kyle's arm in response.

I picked up a large branch, about three feet long, and rushed at him again. I held out the branch like a lance, intending to jam it right through his eye.

Ogre knocked the branch out of my hand then backhanded me across the face. Once again I hit the ground.

"Mommy!" Theresa screamed.

This time, Ogre wasn't going to let me get back up. I saw his huge foot coming down toward my face and rolled out of the way. I tried to sit up but couldn't...his shoe had landed on a large chunk of my hair.

I strained to pull free. I was willing to yank out every strand of hair on my head if that's what it took.

Ogre raised his other foot.

As he looked down at me, a blob of his blood-drool spattered against my cheek.

Kyle's hand suddenly wrapped around Ogre's face, clawing at his eye. "*Leave Mommy alone!*" he screamed.

Ogre momentarily lost his balance. His foot slammed down inches from my face. His feet were now straddling each side of my head.

I reached up between his legs, grabbed tight, and squeezed as hard as I could, using my fingernails.

Ogre cried out.

And then began to *really* lose his balance.

I hurriedly moved out of the way as he lifted the foot that was pinning my hair. He stumbled forward, and then started to fall.

Kyle was going to be crushed beneath him.

They say things move in slow motion during moments where every split second counts, and I found this to be absolutely true. I reached for the arm holding Kyle and raked it with my fingernails, trying to break his grip on my son before he fell.

Ogre's grip did not loosen one iota.

Slow motion transformed back into regular speed as Ogre dropped to the ground.

Landing on his knees and not on my son.

For a terrifying moment I thought he was going to tumble forward onto his stomach, but this time he sustained his balance. Kyle frantically but unsuccessfully tried to pull himself free.

I raked Ogre's arm with my fingernails again.

Kyle leaned down and bit deep into Ogre's flesh.

"Ow, shit!" Ogre screamed, finally letting Kyle go. He shoved him away. "You goddamn little cannibal!"

I punched Ogre in the face as hard as I could. This time he seemed to feel it.

"Kyle, run!" I shouted as Ogre slammed his hands against my shoulders. He stood back up, lifting me along with him.

"How about I grind *your* bones, bitch?" he snarled, squeezing his hands together.

My arms were pinned, but I kicked him over and over. And by now I was filled with so much adrenaline that these kicks were taking their toll. Ogre let me drop then grabbed the back of my neck.

He slammed my face into his gut and pushed hard.

The smell of rotten sweat was almost unbearable.

I couldn't breathe.

Dear God, I was going to suffocate against the belly of a five-hundred pound maniac.

I tried to push away but couldn't. My face was pressed so tightly against his belly that I couldn't open my mouth to bite him.

I landed several blows with my fists that did absolutely no good.

I could feel myself starting to black out.

"You little shit!" Ogre shouted, although his voice seemed to be miles away. "I'll tear your tiny little—"

I could suddenly breathe again.

"—head off!"

As I pulled away, Theresa jabbed the branch into Ogre's ribs once again. He swatted her aside, only to be met by another branch in his other side, wielded by Kyle.

Though neither of the branches had poked right through his body, Ogre had spots of his own blood on his shirt .

Theresa jabbed him again.

So did Kyle.

In one smooth motion, Ogre swung his arms together, catching each of my children and slamming them into each other.

He tossed their dazed bodies aside as I grabbed my own branch and lunged at him again. This time it tore across the side of his head, still missing his eye.

He snatched the stick out of my hand, picked me up, hoisted me over his head like a professional wrestler, and then tossed me into the air. I landed hard next to Kyle and Theresa, sure I'd broken something.

Ogre wiped the blood off the side of his head. "I'm gonna eat all three of you right up," he said, enraged. "I'm your death. I'm the bogeyman." He stepped towards us. "And I like little girl meat the best of all."

My every muscle was aching. My bones felt like eggshells. My blood felt like ignited kerosene. But I still got back up...not in a fluid ballerina-like motion, but back up nevertheless...and put myself between this monster and my children.

Ogre raised his fists and smiled. "You really think you can take me?"

I raised my own fists and gave him a steel-eyed gaze. "No."

"Good. Then we're in agreement."

He stepped toward me and I stepped toward him. We began to slowly circle each other like boxers.

Ogre spat out some blood.

I spat out some of my own.

He was almost five times my size, but I wasn't going to back down.

"I'll hand it to you, you've got some spark," said Ogre, leering at me as if a fight weren't the only thing he had planned.

"I'm pregnant," I told him.

A moment of uncertainly flashed in his eyes.

"That's right. You're beating up on a pregnant lady. I bet that makes you feel like a real man, doesn't it?"

The leer returned. "You know, I said little girl meat was my favorite, but I was wrong. Do you know what *really* tastes the best? Do you know what I most like to feel rolling around on my tongue?"

I ran at him, claws extended, before he could finish.

He batted me aside.

"Yeah, you know what I'm talking about," said Ogre. "Maybe I'll just suck it right out of your belly for dessert."

I felt like I was going to vomit. But no. I couldn't let him get to me. They were just words.

Ogre made a vulgar slurping sound.

I ran at him again.

This time, instead of hitting me, he grabbed my arm and twisted it around my back. I cried out in pain.

"Shhhhh...not so loud, you'll wake the baby," said Ogre.

Out of the corner of my eye I saw something running toward us. Joe.

The pug latched on to Ogre's foot and thrashed around, biting and snarling.

Ogre gave it a kick. Joe let out a high-pitched squeal then attacked his leg again.

It was enough of a distraction. I reached around and grabbed a handful of blubber, digging my fingernails into Ogre's gut.

Theresa, who I hadn't even seen get up, slammed a new branch into Ogre's side.

Ogre released my arm, grabbed my other hand, and pried it off his belly.

Theresa jabbed him again. The tip of the branch broke off in his side.

A second kick, a second squeal, but Joe kept fighting.

Ogre lurched his head down toward my face, mouth wide open, giving me a full blast of his fetid breath.

I leaned out of the way.

He lurched at me again, moving his mouth in an animalistic biting motion. His red teeth clacked together over and over, so viciously I thought he might shatter them.

I swear he growled.

He pushed Theresa out of the way, but she came right back at him, stabbing the branch several inches into his side.

Ogre spun around, practically roaring, and reached for my daughter. I leapt up onto his back, wrapped both of my arms around his neck, and squeezed.

He grabbed my arms and tried to pry them off, but I refused to budge.

Nothing could make me budge.

I squeezed and squeezed, trying to crush his throat.

Ogre staggered away from Theresa, swinging around as he tried to dislodge me. It wasn't going to happen.

I put everything I had, every last bit of strength I possessed in the entire world into breaking his neck.

"I'll kill you!" he screamed.

I wasn't squeezing hard enough if he could still scream.

"I'm gonna...gonna..."

He let out a disgusting choking sound.

He continued to stumble around. My strangulation efforts were clearly doing some good. I couldn't possibly squeeze any harder, but I sure as hell wasn't going to let up.

He moved more and more erratically, swaying back and forth. And in a moment of raw horror I realized where our struggle had taken us.

I let go of him and slipped off his back.

His foot snapped the fishing line.

A long metal spear sailed down from the trees, striking the upper left side of his skull. The tip burst out through his right thigh.

Ogre stood in place for what felt like an endless moment, and then fell.

I stared at him in shock.

Now the forest animals could eat him.

I turned away from the gruesome sight and Theresa rushed into my arms. I gave her a tight hug despite my aching limbs, and we hurried over to Kyle, who still lay on the ground. The bite on his arm was deep, but he wouldn't bleed to death.

I snapped my fingers in front of his face. "Kyle? Are you with me?"

He nodded.

I hugged both of my children. Joe didn't want to be left out, and licked my hand.

"Is the bogeyman dead?" Kyle asked.

"He wasn't the bogeyman," I said. "He was just a big fat loser. And yes, he's dead."

Kyle nodded his understanding.

"You were both very brave," I told them. "And I need you to keep being brave just like that. We're going to help your father. I've got a plan."

Chapter Twelve

It's Andrew again.

"One for you," said Troll, giving me a quick cut on the leg, "and one for me." He cut himself on the leg in the same spot. "One for you, one for me. One for you, one for me."

"Okay, that's enough," said Witch, wrinkling her nose in disgust. "Let's get him back to the truck."

"One for you..."

"I said, that's enough!"

"Sometimes I think you don't appreciate the finer things in life."

"It's a wonder you have any skin left."

"You should see me naked."

"All right, enough! Let's get moving."

Witch kept her gun pointed at me while Troll stood up and pulled me to my feet. "Ready to go for walkies?" he asked.

"No, but I'm ready to crap on your front lawn."

"We don't really have a front lawn."

I almost offered to crap on his shoes, but there have to be minimum standards to even this type of conversation. With Witch keeping me very nicely covered with her gun, I got up and we headed back toward the store.

"So, Troll, is that your real name?" I asked.

Troll chuckled. "Do you always ask such dumb questions?"

"No, I just thought that might be how you guys met. Maybe at a party or something. 'Hi, I'm Troll.' 'No way, I'm Witch!' 'Wow, your parents hated you too, huh?' 'Oh yeah. So, do you want to get together and hunt innocent vacationers in the Georgia shrubbery?' 'Sure, why not?'"

Troll snorted. "Like I said, you're a funny guy."

"Did you get to pick your own names?"

"Yeah."

"That's cool. Otherwise somebody could've gotten stuck with Orc or something. You just don't want to go around saying 'Hi, I'm Orc.' Or maybe Pixie. Why didn't you pick Dragon, though? Dragon would've been much cooler than Troll. When I think Troll, I think of a weasely little hairy thing living under a bridge eating goats."

"You know, Andrew, the only reason I'm letting you yammer on like this is because you're a dead man. Might as well get all the talking in while you still can."

"I disagree," said Witch. "Shut the fuck up."

"You heard the lady," Troll told me.

I stopped talking for the rest of the walk.

⁓⁓

We reached the store and went inside. "Oh, hell no," said Charlie, emerging from the far aisle. "Don't bring him back in here again!"

"He'll be good this time," Troll assured him. "All we want is some duct tape."

"Yeah, right. You shove any more of those candy bars in your pockets and I'll have your self-mutilating ass."

"Oh, waah, waah, waah. Quit being such a baby. When was the last time you had a customer in this place? Jeez, you've got gallons of milk in the cooler that are completely solid. I've seen 'em."

Witch held her walkie-talkie to her mouth. "Goblin, you there?"

"Yeah."

"We're at Charlie's place."

"I'm right around the corner. I'll be there before Troll can steal a pack of Rolos."

"Gotcha. Witch out."

Troll took a new roll of duct tape off one of the shelves and unspooled an armlength of it. "Put out your hands," he told me.

I obliged, if only because Witch hadn't stopped pointing that gun at me. Troll wrapped the duct tape around my wrists several times, binding them together.

"Put some over his mouth," said Witch.

"I don't think they make a roll big enough for that."

"Just do it."

Troll put a long strip of duct tape over my mouth.

A truck pulled into the parking lot outside. The motor turned off, and then Goblin entered the store.

"Oh my goodness," he said, looking at me. "You're looking kind of humble there, Andrew."

I said something amazingly clever that was muffled by the duct tape.

"I'm very glad to see you again," said Goblin. "As I'm sure you know, I've had a really lousy day, and I can't think of any better way to improve it than to watch you get strapped to a table and have your body parts replaced with..." He put his hand over his mouth in mock realization. "Ooops. That's supposed to be a surprise, isn't it?"

"We've got some good ones lined up," said Witch. "Maximum pain."

"That's what I want. I mean, sure, we could just throw him down to the floor right now and stomp him to a bloody pulp, but then, what progress would we have made?"

"You're not stomping a damn thing into a bloody pulp here," said Charlie.

Goblin waved dismissively at him. "Go organize some stock or something."

Charlie opened his mouth as if to say something, but settled for glaring.

"So, Andrew, I'm sorry to hear about your friends," said Goblin. "I hope it was quick."

I said something equally clever that was equally muffled. Troll ripped off the duct tape, and I grimaced in pain.

"What was that?" Goblin asked.

"I said, bite me."

"Good one."

Troll slapped another strip of duct tape over my mouth.

"Anyway, I think we've hung out in this squalor long enough. Let's deliver our new friend Andrew to the lab, shall we?"

Goblin's walkie-talkie crackled. "Is anybody there?" asked a voice I instantly, and joyously, recognized.

"Who is this?" asked Goblin.

"I'm Momma Bear. How about we make a deal?"

Goblin laughed incredulously. "What's with all the deals? You'd think we were brokers or something."

"Shut up and listen. Your large friend here fell down and went boom. What do you say we make a trade?"

"Could you describe this particular friend for me?"

"A quarter ton and lying unconscious at my feet."

"Is that so?" asked Goblin. "Now, you're a petite little thing, aren't you? How exactly did you manage to take out Ogre?"

"I had help. A seven-year-old, a nine-year-old, and a pug."

"I'm sorry, ma'am, I'm having a bit of trouble with that scenario. The klutz dropped his walkie-talkie somewhere, didn't he? I think I'm going to need some proof. Describe the birthmark on his right shoulder."

A few seconds of silence.

"It looks sort of like a deformed butterfly."

"Uh-oh," Troll whispered.

Goblin frowned. "Okay, you've got my attention. What is it you want?"

"I want my husband and my friends back. You let them go, and I'll tell you where to find your buddy."

"I'm afraid I have some bad news for you," said Goblin. "Apparently two members of your party are deceased. Your husband's okay, though."

"Let me talk to him."

"That can possibly be arranged. First, let me hear Ogre."

"He's unconscious."

"I know. But he snores loud enough to wake the dead. Let me hear it."

"He isn't snoring."

"Now, see, we have a bit of a continuity error here, because Ogre *always* snores. Therefore, he must be..." Goblin trailed off as he apparently realized exactly what this meant. "...aw, shit."

Troll slammed his fist against one of the shelves. "What the hell is the matter with us today?"

"Shut up," Goblin snapped at him. He spoke into the walkie-talkie. "I want to share some important information with you, Momma Bear. You're not getting out of these woods, I promise you. I don't mean that as a vague threat, I mean you aren't getting out, case closed. But I'll make you a deal of my own. We're at the store where you all stopped not too long ago, and dear Andrew currently has all ten of his fingers. Every five minutes, the number of fingers will be reduced by one. Then we're going to put a gun in his mouth and make him pull the trigger with one of his bloody stumps. So you've got fifty minutes to get yourself over here and save your husband's life. Does that deal work for you?"

"Let me talk to him."

Troll tore off the tape again. Once more and I was sure the tape would take my lips with it. Goblin held the walkie-talkie to my mouth. I shook my head and refused to speak.

"Say something," Goblin demanded.

I remained silent.

Goblin shrugged, and then kicked me in the leg. I couldn't help but let out a grunt of pain.

"Did that sound like him?" Goblin asked into the walkie-talkie.

"Helen, stay away from here," I said. "They'll kill you. Are the kids okay?"

"Yes, we're still together."

"Don't come anywhere near the store. It's a trap. Get Kyle and Theresa to safety."

"Well, of *course* it's a trap," Goblin said. "The point was to see if true love would get her to risk her life to save yours. Tell me, Witch, has it been five minutes yet?"

"No, but we can cheat."

"Well, we don't want to cheat. That wouldn't be fair. Instead let's tweak the rules and say the clock started at the beginning of this conversation. Troll, find a pair of wire cutters."

"Don't worry about that, I've got my knife."

Goblin shook his head. "It'll be easier with the wire cutters."

"Why make it easy?"

"Because you won't be cutting off his finger." Goblin looked me in the eye. "He'll be doing it to himself."

"Oooooh, kinky," said Troll, laughing as he walked over to the far aisle.

"If you get blood on any tools, you're paying for them," Charlie said. "I mean it."

"Helen, don't come here, no matter what," I said. "Let me talk to the kids!"

"Aw, this is so touching," said Goblin.

"Daddy...?" said Theresa, hesitantly.

"Yes, Theresa, it's Daddy. I love you, sweetheart."

On the other end I heard Theresa burst into tears.

"This is gonna make me sick," said Witch.

"You're right, enough of this sappy crap. Troll, are you going to get those wire cutters or do I have to gnaw his finger off myself?"

"Right here," said Troll, emerging from the aisle, waving a pair of wire cutters still in the package. "Nice and new."

"Who said you could open new merchandise?" Charlie demanded. "This is my store! You people don't get to just help yourselves to whatever you want!"

"Give it a rest, Charlie," said Goblin. "I mean it."

"Hey, we're in my store, and nobody tells me to—"

"*Now!*"

Troll glanced at the back of the package. "Oh, wait, it says here 'Not For Use On Human Fingers.' Doesn't say anything about toes, though."

Goblin snatched the wire cutters out of his hand. "Grow up. Get his hands free." While Troll used his knife to cut the duct tape binding my hands, Goblin removed the wire cutters from the packaging and held them in front of my face. "Well, Andrew, the clock is ticking, so we'd better get started. Are you left handed or right handed?"

"Right." No sense lying.

"Good man. Then I'll let you pinch off your left pinky." He handed me the wire cutters while Witch kept her gun pointed at my face. "Open the jaws."

His expression made it clear he wasn't playing around. I was feeling utterly sick to my stomach, but I opened the jaws of the wire cutters.

"Put them over your finger. All the way down at the bottom."

I wondered if I could slam the wire cutters into Goblin's face without being shot by him, Witch, and/or Troll. It seemed unlikely.

"I'm not cutting off my finger for you," I informed him.

"Oh, I think you will. And your family is going to hear the screams." He jiggled the walkie-talkie.

"Forget it. I'm not doing it."

"Hmmmm...bullet to the face, or missing pinky? I think you'll make the right choice. I'm going to give you until the count of ten. And though you probably remember this from the countdown to the Molotov cocktails in the camper, let me be perfectly clear on something, Andrew: I'm not the kind of person who will say nine-and-a-half."

I believed him.

"So let's get started before it's already time for you to cut a second finger off. Ten...nine..."

The psycho was absolutely serious. If I didn't chop off a finger, I'd be shot in the face.

"...eight...seven...six..."

I put the jaws of the wire cutters over the little finger on my left hand.

"...five..."

I looked Goblin straight in the eye. "I'll kill you for this."

"...four..."

I began to squeeze the handle of the wire cutters. A drop of blood pooled on the blade.

Chapter Thirteen

I type using hunt-and-peck anyway, but losing a finger is a pretty big deal. I winced, sucked in a deep breath, and then...

...the wall of the store exploded.

Well, it didn't really *explode*, not the way the camper exploded. It's more like it broke apart, sending merchandise flying everywhere, as a direct result of the green truck plowing right through it.

Roger was behind the wheel. Samantha was next to him.

A whole bunch of things happened at once, but to be completely honest, I couldn't tell you exactly what they were. I could vaguely sense Troll ducking for cover, and Charlie diving to the floor, and Witch swinging her gun in the direction of the truck, and Goblin nearly getting hit in the face with a jar of baby food.

For myself, the surprise of having a large truck suddenly burst through the wall of the store just in the nick of time to save me from being forced to slice off my pinky caused me to tense up and squeeze the handles of the wire cutters, slicing off my pinky.

"Oh," I said, because sometimes that's all that really needs to be said.

My little finger dropped onto my lap.

Now, I think I've clearly established that I'm not the finest strategist in the world. However, even in my state of shock I knew to take advantage of this situation. I stood up, scooping up my severed finger as I did so, and then threw a punch at Witch with my five-fingered fist.

It was a good one.

I rushed toward the truck, which Roger was quickly backing out of the very large hole he'd created in the store. I felt the blade swish next to my back as Troll took a swipe at me with his knife. As I ran past the passenger-side door, Samantha threw it open, bashing Troll in the chest. She slammed it closed again as I leapt into the back of the truck.

As I ducked down I heard a gunshot and the sound of shattering glass. I took a split second to think about how much my finger stump hurt. I was bleeding all over the place, but at least it wasn't my truck to clean.

The truck pulled out of the store. For an instant I thought I was home free, a pleasant if laughable idea that vanished as soon as Witch jumped into the back of the truck with me.

I immediately dove at her, knocking her off her feet. She punched me in the face approximately as hard as I'd punched her, which was pretty damn hard. Then she swung her gun at me, but I deflected it by grabbing her wrist with my incomplete hand, pinning my severed finger between them.

We struggled for a long moment, me on top, both of us gritting our teeth hard enough to do serious enamel damage, and then a squirt of my blood got her right in the eye. She cried out and instinctively rubbed it while sharing her unladylike vocabulary. I used my other hand to try to wrench the gun out of her grasp, but it wasn't working.

We were now speeding down the dirt road toward Wreitzer Park, a wise decision since the other direction was sort of blocked by an exploded camper and a couple of wrecked trucks. Over the tailgate I could see the other green truck was following us, about a hundred feet behind. The road curved and I lost sight of it.

Finally the gun, now slippery with blood, popped free of both our grips. It slid down the bed of the truck and smacked into the tailgate.

I got in another really good punch.

So did she.

The truck hit a bump, causing Witch's head to bounce up, and then strike the truck bed. Sadly, the hit wasn't hard enough to do anything but piss her off even more.

"You fork!" she screamed. I'm pretty sure that's not what she meant to say, but that's what came out.

Then my finger slipped out of my hand and dropped into her open mouth. Witch did not take this well, gagging and choking and frantically trying to spit it out.

Holy shit, she's going to swallow my finger, I thought, horrified. Surgeons might be able to reattach the digit, but not if it went through her digestive system!

I reached inside her mouth with my good hand, trying to pinch my severed pinky between my index finger and thumb. I could see it at the back of her throat.

Witch bit down.

I cried out in pain and tried to tug free. I couldn't.

Then I clamped my bloody hand over her neck, pushing my thumb into her throat until she let up with her teeth. I pulled my fingers free, but my severed pinky was still in her mouth.

We exchanged another couple of punches.

Witch closed her mouth and I could see her jaw working. She was *chewing* on my finger. This time I clamped my fingers over her nose, trying to force her to open her mouth to take a breath.

The truck took a sharp turn, and I lost my balance and tumbled off of Witch. She sat up, spat out my finger, and picked it up. Then she cocked her hand back as if preparing to fling it out of the moving vehicle.

I grabbed her hand and squeezed tight to make her drop it. She pulled free and elbowed me in the gut, but I quickly tackled her again.

Her forehead bashed against the side of the truck, hard.

She fell over, unconscious.

I picked up my finger and wiped it off on my pants. Despite a few tooth marks, it seemed to be in relatively good shape, at least by severed finger standards. I shoved it into my pocket then scrambled over to the tailgate and retrieved Witch's gun.

Both Witch and I were completely covered in blood, and now that the fight was over I had to admit that I was feeling more than a little dizzy. I crawled back over to Witch, giving a halfhearted smile to Samantha, who was watching me through the rear windshield...and removing her shirt.

Was this supposed to be a reward for vanquishing my foe?

Samantha reached out of the open passenger window and handed her blouse to me. "Wrap up your hand!" she shouted over the sound of the engine.

I took the shirt from her and wrapped it around my injured hand as tightly as I could.

We turned onto a longer stretch of road, and then the other green truck came back into view, close enough that I could see Goblin, Troll, and Charlie inside.

I wondered if they'd be so kind as to let me borrow a cooler in which to store my finger.

Now the dizziness was starting to become a real concern, along with a sudden nausea. At least Roger was the one doing the driving. Perhaps I could take a short nap...?

As we rounded a corner, the brakes squealed.

The tires burst.

And as we careened off the side of the road, I saw we'd driven over one of those "Severe Tire Damage" things with the spikes. The truck took out quite a few bushes and assorted plants before smashing into a tree and coming to a halt.

We had to get out of there. Run into the woods as fast as we could and try to...

Nope. With Samantha's mangled foot, we weren't going anywhere. It wasn't like we could outrun them with Roger carrying her.

Damn.

The other green truck came to a stop right before the tire shredder. Behind me, I heard Roger roll down his window. "So now what?" he asked.

I hoisted Witch's unconscious body into a sitting position and pressed the barrel of the gun against the side of her head.

Goblin and Troll got out of the truck, about thirty feet away from us. Goblin sighed deeply and ran a hand through his hair. "We're playing the hostage game again, aren't we?"

"Uh, yeah," I admitted, sheepishly.

"You have *got* to be kidding me."

"So, you know, if you come any closer I'll kill her and all that, and I want you to let my wife and kids go."

Goblin looked at me, looked at the ground, looked at Troll, sighed deeply, and then looked at me again. "You know what? Fine. That's fine. This isn't worth it anymore. We quit."

"You quit?" I asked, surprised.

"Yeah, we quit. I want to forget this ever happened. We won't hurt your wife and kids. You can even keep the truck, for all I care. Just give us Witch back and get the hell away from us. We won't follow you."

He looked totally serious. Were bad guys allowed to just give up like that?

"How do I know I can trust you?" I asked.

Troll grinned. "We could pinky swear. Oh, wait, I guess not."

Goblin glared at him. "You think this is funny? Does it amuse you to screw up so badly? Because from where I stand, it's pretty damn humiliating."

Troll shrugged. "Whatever."

Goblin returned his attention to me. "So what do you think? Let's just put this all behind us."

"Sounds good to me. But I want my wife and kids back with me first."

"Gee, you think?" Goblin asked, rolling his eyes. He pressed a button on his walkie-talkie. "Momma Bear, are you there?"

"What did you do to my husband?" Helen demanded on the other end.

"Nothing, he's fine. Look, we're just going to call this whole thing off, if that's okay with you. It was a bad idea from the start, and we're all going to cut our losses."

"Let me talk to Andrew."

Goblin extended the walkie-talkie toward me. "Do you want me to toss it to you?"

I couldn't very well catch it with one hand wrapped up in bloody cloth and the other holding a gun to the head of an unconscious psycho. "Uh, no. Roger, you wanna catch the walkie-talkie for me?"

"Have him throw it by the side of the truck."

"It'll break," said Goblin.

"The dirt doesn't look all that hard over here."

"This is a fragile piece of equipment," Goblin insisted. "If I throw it on the ground it might break or the settings might get all messed up and you won't be able to talk to her and we'll never get this resolved."

"Okay, okay, fine." Roger got out of the truck. "Throw it."

Goblin tossed the walkie-talkie over to him. It nearly bounced out of Roger's hands, but he managed to keep a hold on it without looking like too much of an idiot. Then he climbed into the back of the truck with me.

"Here, I'll handle her," he said, trading me the gun for the walkie-talkie. He kept Witch propped up with the gun to her head.

"Helen?" I asked.

"Andrew! Are you okay? What happened?"

"Nothing, this whole thing was just a big misunderstanding. They actually wanted to try to interest us in a multi-level marketing scheme, but they got mixed up and tried to kill us instead."

"Andrew, don't joke."

"Sorry. I think we're okay now. What I need you to do is very carefully lead the kids toward the road. Watch out though, because there are some booby traps out there."

"Believe me, I know."

"How far are you from the road?"

"I'm not sure. Not too far, I hope."

"Let me know when you can see the road, but don't show yourself," I told her.

"Okay. I love you."

"I love you too."

I extended the walkie-talkie toward Goblin, and then, on second thought, drew it back. "Can I keep this for now?"

"Yeah, sure, whatever."

Charlie got out of the truck, apparently satisfied there wasn't going to be any upcoming violence. "You're going to pay for what you did to my store," Charlie shouted, pointing accusingly at Roger. "You don't just drive a truck through a man's place of business and expect to get away with it! You'll be cleaning up my place, and you'll be doing it without any fingers on your hands, I promise you that!"

"Shut up, Charlie," said Troll.

"I don't have to shut up! That store is my livelihood! It's bad enough that I've got you shoplifting all the damn time and I have to watch your unnatural perversions, but now my store is ruined! Did you miss the truck breaking through the wall? Did you see how much merchandise was damaged? You think I get that stuff for free? You think some delivery guy just stops by and says 'Here you go, compliments of the house,'? You think I don't have bills to pay? Debts to settle? Pets to feed?"

Goblin pointed his gun at Charlie's head. "Okay, I'm *not* in the mood for you right now. Shut up."

"You shut up! You think what you're paying me to help you guys out is going to cover the damage to my store? I'm tired of this! This is horseshit! Hell, I probably won't even be *able* to get it fixed because you whack-jobs will kidnap and murder the laborers! Screw you all!"

Troll took out his own gun. "Charlie, I highly recommend that you give your mouth a rest."

"All of you! Screw you!"

Goblin and Troll both pulled their triggers at the same time. Goblin's bullet hit him in the forehead, while Troll's struck him in the nose...or maybe it was the other way around. Either way, there wasn't much left of Charlie's head as his body dropped to the ground.

"Shut...the...fuck...up!" Goblin shouted, firing a bullet into Charlie's lifeless body in between each word. "What the hell do I have to do to get you to shut up?"

"That may have worked," Troll noted.

"I *know* the truck broke through his store! I saw it happen! We all have problems today! Give me a break!" Goblin wiped some spittle off on his sleeve. "I should've stayed in bed this morning."

Roger and I just gaped at him.

"What are you looking at?" Goblin demanded.

I pressed the black button on the walkie-talkie. "Helen? Still try to be careful of booby traps, but you might want to hurry."

Chapter Fourteen

"How's your foot?" I asked Samantha.

"Hurts," she said. "How's your hand?"

"Hurts."

"Sorry."

"Me too."

I avoided turning around to look at her. Something about having my best friend's well-endowed girlfriend sitting behind me wearing only a bra made me a bit uncomfortable. It seemed odd that I was bruised, battered, cut, missing a finger, covered in blood, and yet still unnerved by an awkward social situation, but there you go.

At least I could still joke about it.

"So, she's wearing my pants and I'm wearing her blouse," I said, holding up my wrapped hand to show Roger. "Not many best friends are as generous as you."

Roger chuckled. "Yeah, well, don't try cutting off another finger to see more."

I shrugged. "It might be worth it."

"Guys, I'm right here," said Samantha, amused.

I was keeping tight pressure on my hand and was pretty sure I wouldn't bleed to death if we managed to resolve all of this unpleasantness soon. The idea that I had my own finger in my pocket seriously creeped me out, so I tried not to think about it.

"I know we're supposed to do a lot of macho posturing," said Roger, "but I'm really glad you're not dead."

"Thanks. I'm glad you're not dead, too."

"Thanks."

"I do sort of wish Goblin and Troll were dead."

"That's understandable."

Goblin and Troll were sitting in their truck, looking generally unhappy.

"So how did you get the keys to the truck?" I asked.

"We didn't. Samantha hotwired it."

I turned around to glance at her through the rear windshield. "You know how to hotwire a truck?"

She nodded. "An important skill in the fashion business."

I turned back to Roger. "Wow. I'm impressed."

"Well, she's a pretty special lady," said Roger, giving me a look.

I wanted to say *don't give me that look*, but I couldn't with Samantha around. She really was a pretty special lady.

Suddenly, sitting in the back of a wrecked truck with one of my fingers newly severed and Roger sitting next to me holding the gun to the head of an unconscious psychopath, I realized why I didn't like Samantha.

It wasn't that she wasn't good enough for Roger. It was that she was *perfect* for him. I didn't dislike her. I was just scared she'd take Roger away from me.

I was worried that instead of hanging out with me at the Java Joint on Wednesday nights, Roger would be stuck at home, hanging up laundry and giving foot massages.

I didn't have introspective moments very often (apart from those involving television shows), so this was a rather amazing revelation.

It was an amazingly *pathetic* revelation.

I mean, I had a wife and two frickin' kids, with a third on the way, and I still found time to bum around. What was I worried about?

"It's going to be okay," I told Roger, giving him a look, although a different look than the one he'd given me. "Everything."

"Everything what?"

"You know. Everything."

Roger stared at me. "Huh?"

"Never mind."

"Okay."

"So what made you decide to follow me?"

"We thought you might need help. It happens a lot."

"It does not."

"Sure it does."

I shook my head. "Actually, if I remember correctly, and I think I do, it's *you* who generally needs saving."

"That's not true."

"Which one of us got strapped to that machine that was going to chop off his arms, legs, and head?"

"Which one of us was responsible for me being strapped to that machine that was going to chop off my arms, legs, and head?"

"We weren't discussing responsibility. We were discussing the need to be rescued."

"You were trapped in that giant plastic cube with the darts," Roger pointed out.

"You're right. That cube sucked."

"Anyway, Samantha and I decided we weren't doing any good just sitting around, so I carried her back to the store. We saw that you were in deep ka-ka and decided to save you."

"By crashing through the store."

"Yep."

"Did you consider the possibility that by doing that, you might run me over?"

"It was an irony I was willing to accept," said Roger with a grin.

"Well, that's soothing."

"I thought you'd like that."

"You know what else is ironic? The last time we were at the Java Joint, this lady offered me a hundred thousand dollars to deliver a suitcase to Arizona. I turned her down. I thought it carried the risk of causing problems in my life."

"You turned down a hundred grand without asking me first?"

"I was being responsible!"

"Screw responsibility! Responsibility gets your pinky chopped off. Take the money."

"Well, I know that now." I nodded toward Witch. "How's she doing?"

"Still zonked."

I pressed the black button on the walkie-talkie. "Helen, how's it going?"

"I think we're getting there."

"Sounds good." I set down the walkie-talkie.

Goblin got out of the truck and stepped over the tire shredder. "We've got ourselves a bit of a problem, gentlemen."

"What's that?"

"The alert signal just went off. Somebody's coming down the road."

"How far away?"

"About five minutes. We all just need to play it cool. Whoever it is, we'll tell them everything's all right, we've already contacted the police about your accident, and we'll let them drive on through."

"Sounds good," I said, gesturing to my blood-covered shirtless body. "They'll never suspect a thing."

"There's some bottled water under the seat," Goblin told me. "Get yourself cleaned up as much as you can. This doesn't have to turn into a bloodbath if we all play it right."

I almost mentioned the exploded camper, but caught myself in time. If Goblin didn't remember that the wreckage was down the road, I certainly wasn't going to remind him. If I was lucky (which I usually wasn't), whoever drove on through would call the cops when they saw it.

Goblin turned around and motioned for Troll to get out of the truck. Together they began to move the tire shredder off to the side of the road.

"What should we do about her?" Roger asked me, gently tapping his gun against Witch's head.

"Do we have anything to cover her with?"

"I could keep up with the trend of the day and use my shirt."

"You know, that's a great opening for a fat joke, but actually you've lost a bit of weight since you started dating Samantha."

"You noticed?"

"Yeah, but I didn't want to say anything because, you know, we're guys and stuff."

Samantha reached out of the truck window and handed me a bottled water. "Just carry her out into the woods."

"We can't leave her," I said. "What if she wakes up?"

"Then don't leave her. Hide out there with her."

I unscrewed the cap and poured the warm water over my shoulders and chest. "We can't leave you, either."

"Then don't leave me," said Samantha, as if speaking to a remarkably stupid child. Many people have spoken to me in that tone of voice over the years. When we finally made it home I'd have to look into improving my intelligence level. "We'll all hide out there."

"Okay," I said, emptying the rest of the bottle. There were still streaks of blood on me, but that wouldn't matter if we were hiding out in the woods. "Roger, you carry her out there, and I'll keep our friends covered with the gun. Witch should be okay for a minute while you come back and get Samantha."

"Sounds good," said Roger, handing me the gun. Goblin and Troll had dragged Charlie's corpse out of sight and now Goblin was in their truck, driving it off to the side of the road so the approaching vehicle could get past. Troll was scattering dirt on the remnants of Charlie remaining on the road.

Roger got out of the truck, and then reached into the back and picked up Witch, putting one arm under her knees and one behind her back.

Had she stirred just a bit?

Nah.

Roger lifted her out of the truck and walked toward the woods.

"What are you doing?" Goblin demanded.

"We can't have her just lying in the back of the truck," I said.

"This part of the woods is *loaded* with traps! If you want to march through there, be my guest, but if you try to bring her with you the deal is off. I didn't swallow my pride just to have her ripped up by three dozen rusty poison darts."

Roger hesitated.

Troll looked at his watch. "You'd better decide either way. We don't know how fast they're driving."

"Let's put her inside the truck," said Roger. Samantha opened the door for him and he not-so-gently set Witch inside in an upright position. Then he and I got into the truck as well, brushing safety glass off the seat from the shattered windshield, the four of us tightly squeezed together. I looked over my shoulder and saw Troll get into his own truck with Goblin.

"Shouldn't we have worked out a cover story first?" asked Samantha. "What if the people stop and want to know what happened?"

"I think we're going to have to wing it," I noted, as I heard the sound of a vehicle approaching.

Witch twitched.

Then coughed.

The vehicle, a dirty but impressive black limousine, came around the corner. It began to slow down.

Roger grabbed Witch by the collar and yanked her down, bashing her forehead against the dashboard. She jabbed him in the side with her elbow, and he yanked her down again, bashing her forehead once more.

The limousine came to a stop right next to our truck. The windows were tinted, preventing us from seeing who was inside.

"*I'll kill you!*" Witch screamed, lashing out at both Roger and Samantha. They struggled to keep her under control.

I reached past Roger and pushed the gun into her side. Witch seemed unaware of it and kept up her violent flailing.

The Limo's door opened.

"Stop it or I'll shoot!" I whispered.

She didn't seem to hear me.

"Stop it or he'll shoot!" said Samantha, taking her own turn at bashing Witch against the dashboard.

Witch seemed to hear that one. She settled down just as the driver got out.

It was a woman. Early thirties. Attractive. Wearing a red blouse and skirt. Red sensible shoes. Perfect hair and makeup. She grabbed a red leather purse as she exited the vehicle.

Our bloodied, dismembered, mangled, bruised, sweaty, and exhausted group tried to look nonchalant.

"Is everything...okay?" the woman asked.

I nodded and leaned out the window. "Everything's cool. We just had a small accident. We've called the police and they're on their way."

"Looks like a *big* accident."

"Well, yeah. But it was an old truck."

The woman bit her lip. "Look, I don't want to intrude on anybody's business, but are you sure everything's okay? I mean, I saw what happened with...you know, what happened to the woman."

I tried to force a smile. "They were just roughhousing. It's a dysfunctional family."

"I guess."

"Really, we're okay. Just waiting for the cops."

"It's kind of hot for all of you to be crunched together in the truck like that."

"Yeah, but the bugs were eating us alive out there."

"But your windshield is broken and your windows are down.

Y'know, I have a first aid kit in my trunk. All of you look like you could use some patching up."

"That's all right," I insisted. "Like I said, we're just waiting for the cops."

I glanced over at the other truck. Goblin and Troll were watching the scene, carefully.

"You don't even want to borrow a Band-Aid?" the woman asked, eyeing me suspiciously.

I heard a pair of doors open. I looked over and saw Goblin and Troll getting out of their truck.

"Actually, a bandage would be great," I said, opening the door to our truck and sliding out.

"Oh my God, what happened to your hand?" asked the woman.

"Lost a finger."

"Oh my God! Do you still have it? Where is it?"

"In my pocket."

The woman gaped at me. "You have your finger in your pocket?"

I nodded.

"You can't do that! You have to keep it clean! I've got a small cooler in my car with a couple of Cokes, so we'll put it in there until the police get here. What in the world were you thinking?"

Goblin and Troll were walking toward us.

"Ma'am, I appreciate your trying to help, but we're fine. Really."

"You're *not* fine! You're probably in shock. You need to lie down. I'll get my first aid kit and we'll fix you up as much as we can."

I was feeling myself begin to panic, so I gave her a cold stare. "Ma'am, please, mind your own business," I said, trying to sound threatening.

"I beg your pardon?"

"Get out of here. We don't want your help."

The woman looked over at Goblin and Troll and seemed to realize her help was, indeed, not wanted. "Okay. I understand." She unzipped her purse. "Let me at least give you a Band-Aid, for God's sake. I've got one in here."

"I don't need one," I said.

"Don't be rude," Goblin told me, walking up right next to the woman. "Let her give you a Band-Aid."

Troll ran his finger along the blade of his knife.

"Ma'am, please get back in your car before—"

I saw the gun an instant before it went off.

The tiny dart, a red one, protruded from my stomach. The pain was absolutely incredible, instantly searing through my entire body like a fireball. Without hesitating, the woman walked out of my line of sight.

Some commotion, a scream from Samantha, and two more shots.

I fell to my knees. The pain quickly gave way to numbness.

88 JEFF STRAND

"*Nice* shooting," said Troll with a grin as the woman walked back in front of me.

"Thanks," said the woman, not returning his grin. She calmly placed the dart gun back into her purse and straightened her skirt.

My arms and legs were completely stiff. I couldn't even move my fingers...those that were left.

The back door of the limousine opened.

Troll's grin vanished as the occupant stepped out and walked around the front of the car. He was a tall, well-built man in his forties, wearing an immaculate grey suit.

He did not look happy.

Chapter Fifteen

The man stroked his thin, black goatee and looked first at me, and then at the wrecked truck. "Do they have any weapons?" he asked Goblin.

"The guy in the truck has a gun," Goblin said. "But I can explain—"

"And you will. Surprised it was me and not a new set of victims, were you? I heard some very interesting things over your walkie-talkie chatter. Medusa, retrieve the gun."

The woman in red nodded and calmly walked over to the truck.

The man regarded me with distaste. "He looks pathetic."

"Yeah," said Goblin, trying to smile. "We took care of him pretty well."

"You took care of *nothing*!" the man said, pointing an accusing finger at Goblin. "Where are Ghoul and Ogre?"

Goblin was silent for a moment. "They're...I mean, you've already heard, right?"

"I want to hear it directly from your mouth."

"They're dead."

"And who killed them?" The man gestured to me. "Him?"

Goblin shook his head. "His wife."

"Oh, his wife, was it? Well, at least you took care of the problem. Please, direct me to her corpse so I can spit on it."

"Mr. Burke—"

"I'm 'Sir' to you right now."

"Sir, it wasn't our fault."

"Oh, I'm glad to hear that. I can only assume the hand of God Himself reached down and pulled her to safety."

Medusa handed the gun she'd taken from Roger to Mr. Burke.

"This is one of yours," he said, glancing down at the weapon.

"Yes, sir."

"Have we decided to start arming our victims? Is that it?"

"No, sir."

"Let me explain something to you, Goblin. I do not like being forced to micromanage what you are doing out here. When I am forced to leave my lab to clean up your messes, it wastes my time and causes me to become extremely annoyed. Do you understand?"

"Yes, sir."

"From what I understand of this ill-fated project, there were six people in the camper you ambushed. How many of them did you bring to me?"

Goblin was silent.

"How many?"

"None."

"How many of their corpses did you bring to me?"

"None."

"And how many of them were young, helpless children?"

"Sir, I—"

"Answer the question."

"Two."

"Two young children. And yet through your incompetence, your staff has now been reduced by forty percent. I don't like that kind of attrition, Goblin."

"I'm sorry."

"In fact, there's very little I *do* like at this moment. I'm terminating this branch of the project, effective immediately."

Goblin didn't bother to protest.

I desperately tried to make my body work...any part of it...but I remained a human statue.

Mr. Burke furrowed his brow. "Is that Ghoul's body?" he asked, pointing at the corpse by the side of the road.

"Uh, no," Goblin admitted. "It's Charlie."

"They killed Charlie, too?"

Goblin started to nod, but then apparently thought better of the lie. "No, sir, we did."

"We?"

"Troll and I."

Troll shifted uncomfortably.

"You murdered one of our accomplices?"

"Yes, sir."

"Would it be terribly inconvenient if I asked you why?"

"He wouldn't shut up."

"I see. He did like to ramble on. So essentially, you're telling me that under your management, excessive talking is an infraction punishable by death, correct?"

"Sir, we weren't thinking straight."

"That doesn't matter. As a good manager, I have no doubt you accept full responsibility for your actions. And you're telling me you consider excessive talking a fatal offense, correct? One worth terminating a member of your own team?"

"He wasn't really part of the team."

"A vendor, then. You'd terminate a vendor for excessive talking.

That does leave me to wonder about the appropriate punishment for a manager who screwed up a project so badly it left two of his associates dead and none of his goals achieved."

Now Goblin seemed close to tears. "Sir, please, I'll go after the woman and children myself. I'll personally bring them to you, I swear."

"And you'll bring Ghoul, Ogre, and Charlie back to life?"

Goblin seemed unsure how to respond.

"How about just Ogre? If you'll bring Ogre back from the dead, perhaps I'll show you some mercy."

"Sir, I can't—"

"I don't like to hear the word 'can't,' Goblin. You know that."

"Just give me one more chance."

"I don't think so. Consider yourself downsized."

Medusa swiftly removed the dart gun from her purse and fired a shot into Goblin's neck. He dropped to the ground.

Mr. Burke crouched down next to Goblin. "Enjoy the lack of sensation while you can. I am going to make you hurt so badly you'll wish your mother had been skinned alive by your father before they had a chance to conceive you."

Troll looked terrified. Mr. Burke stood up and glared at him. "I'm not going to hold you responsible for the incompetence of your supervisor," he said. "But understand me, if you screw up again, you will *not* find the pain pleasurable."

"Yes, sir," said Troll, visibly relieved.

Witch walked into my line of sight, legs wobbling a bit. "Sir, I am so very sorry."

"I'm not impressed by apologies," said Mr. Burke. "And I'm particularly unimpressed by employees who are kidnapped by their own prey. I'll decide your fate within the next two minutes."

Witch lowered her eyes and nodded.

"Now, let's see about tying up some of our loose ends, shall we?" Mr. Burke unclipped a walkie-talkie from his belt, turned a dial, and then pressed the black button on the side. "Is anybody there?"

"Who is this?" I heard Helen say.

"This is Officer Trevor Clemens from the Georgia State Patrol. We've managed to subdue the assailants who attacked you and your family, but your husband has been very badly injured. Could you give us your location?"

"What happened to him?" Helen sounded frantic.

"He's been cut. He's been cut bad, ma'am. We can't move him until the ambulance gets here. Are you near the road?"

"I'm...I'm not sure," Helen admitted.

"Are you lost?"

"I think so."

"That's not a problem, ma'am. We'll get you out of there. Do me a big favor and give us a shout, okay?"

A moment of silence.

I wanted to scream for her to remain quiet, but I couldn't move my lips.

"Let me talk to him," Helen said.

"Ma'am, he's unconscious and losing blood fast. I'm not trying to scare you, and I promise we're doing everything we can, but he may not have much time left."

"Shout out to me," said Helen. "I'll follow your voice."

Mr. Burke lowered the walkie-talkie. "*Hellooooooooooo!*" he shouted. He lifted the walkie-talkie to his mouth again. "Did you hear that?"

"No. God, we must have gotten turned around somehow."

Mr. Burke reached down and picked up Goblin's gun. He fired it into the air. "What about that?"

"Yes, I heard it."

"Are we close?"

"No, but that helped. I know which direction to go at least."

"Then hurry. Get here as quickly as you can. We'll send a search party after you if you're not here by the time reinforcements arrive."

He released the button on the walkie-talkie, and then turned to Troll. "I assume your truck is still in working condition?"

Troll nodded.

"Did you suddenly turn into a mute?"

"No, sir. I mean, I meant yes, sir. The truck works, sir."

"Then put everybody in the back. Including your ex-supervisor."

"Yes, sir."

Troll put his hands underneath Goblin's arms and began to drag him toward the truck. He seemed very pleased to be doing it.

Mr. Burke knelt down next to me. "Creepy, isn't it? Not being able to move like that? I tested it out on myself once and it freaked me out."

"Oh, shit!" Troll exclaimed as he reached the truck.

"What?"

"The signal just went off. Somebody's coming. Same direction that you came."

"Busy little road today. But that's fine. Without incompetent management running the show, we should be able to take care of them without much effort. Medusa, Witch, I want our three test subjects propped up against the truck," Mr. Burke said. "Based on what they've seen so far, they probably think we're all bumbling idiots, a joke. I want them to see very clearly that we are no joke."

Medusa and Witch dragged me over to the truck. I was unable to feel a thing as I slid over the dirt.

Within a couple of minutes, Roger and Samantha were sitting next to me.

I had to do something to save the people who were coming, but what? I couldn't even wiggle a toe.

It seemed like hours before the car, a small white sedan, arrived. It stopped behind the limousine.

Mr. Burke walked over to them. "Hi there," he said, as the driver rolled down his window. "We've had a bit of bad luck and I was wondering if we could get your assistance."

"Of course," said the driver, a cheerful-looking blond guy in his late thirties. He was badly sunburnt and wearing sunglasses. "What's the problem?"

"Car trouble."

"Oh, man, that's always miserable. This is, like, our first vacation without a flat tire or running out of gas or something like that." The driver grinned. "We probably cursed you. Sweet limo you've got there, though."

Don't get out of your car don't get out of your car please don't get out of your car.

The blonde guy opened his car door and got out.

"Right over here," said Mr. Burke, leading him past the limousine. Two more doors opened on the sedan, and a beautiful woman, probably the guy's wife, got out, along with their son, who looked eleven or twelve.

Please no...

The blonde guy frowned a bit and removed his sunglasses as he saw Roger, Samantha and I propped up against the truck. We had to look like zombies, or at least stoned out of our minds.

"What happened to them?" he asked.

"Shock," said Mr. Burke. "As you can see, there was a terrible accident. We tried to call the police, but we seem to be having trouble with our cell phone."

The blonde guy was joined by his wife and son. "We've got one in the car. Alex, why don't you go grab it?"

"No, that won't be necessary," Mr. Burke said. "I'd just like to give you a brief preamble, if I may. What you're going to see in a moment will frighten you very badly, and if you scream, you will die. So don't scream."

Medusa casually pointed Goblin's gun at the family. The mother gasped but didn't scream.

"Excellent. You're off to a good start. Two of my associates will see that the noise and struggling are kept to a minimum, so please cooperate."

Witch and Troll quickly bound each of the family members' hands with duct tape. They also covered the woman and boy's mouths. After they were done, Mr. Burke nodded his approval and walked over to the family. "What's your name?" he asked the blond guy.

"Jim," he softly replied.

"Full name, please."

"Jim Kenyon."

"James, correct?"

"Yes. James Kenyon."

"And is this your wife?"

"Yes."

"Her name?"

"Heather."

"Pleased to meet you, Heather. And this must be your son. You said his name was Alex, right?"

"Yes," said James, his voice quivering.

"Was Alex born in wedlock?"

"Yes."

"Good. Heather, Alex, please drop to your knees."

Heather and Alex, both crying and shaking with fear, did as they were told.

I focused every possible bit of mental energy I possessed on trying to move my body. A finger. A lip. Anything.

"Heather looks like a fine woman, James," said Mr. Burke. "Is everything working out? No problems in your marriage?"

"Yes."

Mr. Burke chuckled. "I apologize. That wasn't a very well-phrased question. Are there any problems in your marriage?"

"No."

"Good, good. How about with young Alex there? Is he doing well in school?"

"Yes."

"Is he into sports? He looks like he'd be into sports."

"Yes."

"Which one?"

"Basketball."

"Really? He seems a bit short for that. I would have thought baseball or soccer. Does he get a lot of game time or does he spend most of it on the bench?"

"He plays."

"Very impressive. You look like a nice, happy family. You're a very lucky man, James, to have such a wonderful wife and son. That does bring up the important question, though: Which of them do you like better?"

"What?"

"I'm not going to beat around the bush here, James. One of them is going to die within the next minute or so. You're going to make the choice."

Move, damn it, move!

I could beat whatever had been in the dart. Mind over matter. I'd break free of this. I focused so hard it felt like my brain was going to burst inside my skull.

"Now, before you speak, I know exactly what you're going to say. You're going to ask me to kill you instead. I hate that. I'm sick of it. If you try to be a martyr, I'll kill both of them. If you don't make the choice in a timely fashion, I'll kill both of them. My hope is that you won't be the type of coward who would let both his wife and child die because he couldn't make a simple decision."

"Please don't do this," said the man in a soft, scared voice.

"It will be a bullet to the back of the head, execution-style. Painless, as far as I know, not having been through that experience myself. Which one dies, James? Heather or Alex? Make the choice."

"I can't..."

Move move move!

"Make the choice, James. Be a man."

Heather and Alex were both sobbing.

"Five seconds until they both die. And you're going to be really disappointed if you think I'm bluffing."

James let out a whimper, and finally choked out the word: "Her."

"Her?"

James nodded, tears gushing down his face.

"Her meaning Heather? You want me to execute Heather instead of Alex?"

Heather let out a muffled wail.

James nodded.

"Say it," Mr. Burke told him.

"I can't."

"Yes, you can. Say 'I want you to kill my wife Heather.'"

"No!"

"You were man enough to make the choice, James. Don't fuck it up because you won't speak the words."

My finger moved. I swore my finger moved.

"I...I want you to...I want you to..."

"It's not that difficult, James."

"I want you to..."

If I could move a finger, I could move my whole body. I could tackle that sadistic son of a bitch and rip his heart out of his chest.

"Say it, James, or they both die!"

"I want you to kill Heather!"

"See, that wasn't so hard, now was it?" Mr. Burke grinned and motioned to Medusa.

She shoved the barrel of her gun against the back of Alex's head, not Heather's...

I can break free of this I can break free I can I can I can!

...and pulled the trigger.

I couldn't look away. I couldn't even blink.

The twelve year-old boy pitched forward onto the dirt.

"Do you see what we did, James?" asked Mr. Burke. "We killed your son instead. Now you get to spend the rest of your life with poor Heather knowing you didn't pick her. You think there'll be problems in the marriage *now*, James?"

Troll laughed.

James didn't respond. His eyes looked dead.

Mr. Burke raised the walkie-talkie to his mouth and pressed the button. "Did you hear that shot?" he asked.

"Yes, it still sounds pretty far," Helen told him, "but we're moving as fast as we can."

"Very good." He lowered the walkie-talkie and stroked his goatee. "I'm not a completely inhuman gentleman, James. I know that what you must be feeling now is a million times worse than any physical agony I could inflict upon you. So, I'm going to show you some mercy. Instead of making you live with your choice, I'm going to finish both of you off in an excruciatingly painful manner. Sound good?"

"Can I do it?" asked Troll, holding up his hunting knife.

Mr. Burke considered that. "Yes, but you only get five minutes to do both of them."

"Mind if I slit his throat and spend the rest of the time with her?"

Mr. Burke nodded. "That's fine. But slit his throat at the end so he can watch."

"I can do that."

"And tape his mouth. Let's avoid noise pollution as much as possible."

Troll turned toward me, smiled, and waved his knife in front of my face. "Watch how creative I can be."

I watched it all, screaming at my body to move the entire time.

Mr. Burke was feeling generous and gave Troll an extra minute.

Chapter Sixteen

Helen's Side

"Chocolate cake with about a gallon of chocolate syrup poured over the top," I said. "What about you, Kyle?"

"I don't know."

"Sure you do. You can have anything in the entire whole wide world to eat when we get out of here. So what sounds really, really good?"

"Nothing."

I was desperately trying to keep my children alert and happy. Word games hadn't been effective, so I'd switched the subject to food.

We walked slowly through the forest, Theresa following right behind me with her hands on my waist, and Kyle completing the human chain with his hands on his sister's waist. I tried to keep my tone of voice cheerful, but I also kept a close eye on every single step we took, watching for traps.

Joe ran alongside of us. I'd carried the pug for a while, but he'd gotten too heavy and I let him go. On one hand, I didn't want my children to be traumatized by the sight of their beloved pet getting killed in a trap, but on the other hand, I'd rather have Joe accidentally run into a trap than us. And at this point, what was one more trauma?

"C'mon, Kyle, any food in the world. If you don't pick one, I'll make you eat broccoli!"

"Yuck," said Theresa.

"That's right, yuck. And it will be the biggest piece of broccoli you've ever seen. Covered with turds."

I was not the type of parent who normally joked about excrement with her children, but I really needed to keep their minds occupied.

"Mommy, my arm hurts," said Kyle.

"I know it does, sweetie. I promise, we'll get you to a doctor who will make it all better. For now you just have to be my brave little boy, okay?"

"Okay," Kyle said without enthusiasm.

"Now are you going to pick a food or do I have to cook you a turd-covered piece of broccoli?"

"Maybe a mammoth," said Kyle.

"A wooly mammoth?"

"Yeah."

"Do you want mammoth steak or mammoth stew?"

Kyle thought for a moment. "I want mammoth pizza."

"All right, it's a nice wooly mammoth pizza for Kyle as soon as we get out of here."

What frightened me was that I didn't know when that would happen. We were admittedly taking it slow, but still, we'd been walking for an awful long time to not have reached the road yet. I wondered if we were lost.

"Can I have mammoth pizza, too?" asked Theresa.

"Sure. Have you ever seen a mammoth? Even Kyle couldn't eat a whole mammoth pizza all by himself."

"And he's a big snorty pig."

"I am not!"

"Are too!"

For the first time in my life, I welcomed a conversation like that from my children. But it stopped as Theresa's voice turned serious. "Mommy, are we going to die?"

"No," I told her. "We're not."

"I'm scared that we are."

"It's okay to be scared, sweetie. But we're not going to die, I promise you."

"What if the man who bit Kyle had diseases?"

"Theresa!"

"Well, what if he did?"

"Theresa Mayhem, stop talking like that. Your brother is going to be fine. The man didn't have any diseases, and he'll never come after us again, and none of us are going to die."

"Do you think I have rabies?" asked Kyle.

"No! Damn it, Theresa, see what you did? Kyle, you don't have rabies. You don't have any disease. Your arm got bit really bad, and I know it hurts, but it's going to be fine. There are no diseases you can catch from a human bite."

As a parent, I tried to never lie to my children. Sure, Andrew and I did the whole Santa Claus, Easter Bunny, and Tooth Fairy thing, but for the most part I tried to speak honestly and directly with them. This wasn't one of those times. I was scared shitless that Kyle might have caught something from that monster's bite, but I couldn't let my son's overactive imagination go rampant right now. I had to keep them calm.

But when Kyle finally did make it to a hospital, he was going to get every test in existence.

"I don't think you know," said Theresa, softly.

I successfully—but only barely—fought back tears.

The walkie-talkie crackled.

"Is anybody there?" an unfamiliar voice asked.

"Who is this?" I asked.

"This is Officer Trevor Clemens from the Georgia State Patrol. We've managed to subdue the assailants who attacked you and your family, but your husband has been very badly injured. Could you give us your location?"

"What happened to him?" I tried not to sound frantic.

"He's been cut. He's been cut bad, ma'am. We can't move him until the ambulance gets here. Are you near the road?"

"I'm...I'm not sure," I admitted.

"Are you lost?"

"I think so."

"That's not a problem, ma'am. We'll get you out of there. Do me a big favor and give us a shout, okay?"

I'm a bit embarrassed to admit I almost did it. I opened my mouth, took a deep breath...and then drew the obvious conclusion that I might not *really* be talking to an Officer Trevor Clemens.

"Let me talk to him," I said.

"Ma'am, he's unconscious and losing blood fast. I'm not trying to scare you, and I promise we're doing everything we can, but he may not have much time left."

"Shout out to me," I told him. "I'll follow your voice."

I listened carefully.

Nothing.

"Did you hear that?"

"No."

Now a gunshot, far off in the distance.

"What about that?"

"Yes, I heard it."

"Are we close?"

"No, but I know which direction to go at least."

"Then hurry. Get here as quickly as you can. We'll be waiting."

There was something vaguely sinister in the way he said "We'll be waiting." My gut told me I wasn't speaking to a police officer. I'm sure I could've asked some appropriate questions and figured this out for sure, but then I'd risk letting him know what I knew...or at least suspected.

But whether I was talking to a killer or a cop, one thing was certain: Andrew's situation was not good.

Was he really cut and bleeding to death?

Or perhaps already dead?

I needed to put that out of my mind. Andrew was one hell of a resilient guy. He'd be fine. He could be superglued to a nuclear warhead and he'd find a way out of it. I had to worry about getting Theresa and Kyle to safety.

But I also wondered if I should leave them behind. Find a good hiding spot for them and head off on my own. I could move more quickly that way (though still carefully) and not run the risk of taking them right back into the hands of the killers.

What if I couldn't find them again?

They'd be found. We'd call the police, have search helicopters fly overhead, and rescue them. We couldn't possibly be *that* far into the woods.

What if the killers found them first?

Or even a wild animal?

I couldn't do it. I couldn't leave them behind. Kyle had almost been taken from me, and I wasn't going to let him out of my sight again. Hell, aside from restroom and shower breaks, he might stay under my watchful eye until he was eighteen.

We continued walking. Though I did my best to stop obsessing over it, I was too distracted with thoughts of Andrew to continue playing word games with my children, so we walked in silence.

At least I knew we were going the right way.

≈≈

Just as I was starting to unconsciously grow comfortable walking through the woods, I saw another fishing line. We gave it a wide berth.

Something moved next to us.

I gasped and stopped in my tracks. Theresa walked into my back. "Mommy!"

"Shhh!" I listened carefully.

"What was that?" asked Kyle.

"Shhh!" I repeated.

"Is it them?"

"Kyle, be quiet!" We stood there, listening.

Branches crackled.

My stomach lurched.

The deer bounded past, about thirty feet away. It was gone before I could even get a clear look.

"What is that?" Kyle asked, his voice on the verge of panic.

"It was just a deer," I assured him.

"I didn't see it! Are you sure that's what it was?"

"I'm positive. Theresa, did you see it?"

"Uh-huh."

"Tell Kyle it was just a deer."

"It was just a deer, stupid."

"Oh," said Kyle, uncharacteristically ignoring the "stupid" comment.

"I hope it doesn't get killed in a trap," Theresa said.

"It won't. It'll be fine. Come on, let's keep going."

We continued walking through the woods.

I kept my hands in front of me so that my kids couldn't see that they were trembling.

⁓⁓

"Is that the road?" Theresa asked.

It looked that way. I had to force myself to maintain our careful pace. It felt like we'd been walking for hours, though I was sure it wasn't nearly that long, and I didn't want to get us killed in a last-minute rush.

But as we got closer, I could see that yes, we were indeed approaching the dirt road.

Or *a* dirt road, anyway.

A few minutes later we emerged from the woods. I couldn't tell for certain, but it did seem to be the same dirt road we'd been on before. I raised the walkie-talkie to my lips and pressed the black button. "Hello?"

No response.

"Hello?" I asked again. "Is anybody there?"

Still nothing.

That didn't really mean anything. I could be out of walkie-talkie range, or the cop/murderer might not have it on him.

At this point, there wasn't much we could do but walk along the side of the road. At least now we could pick up the pace without worrying about death traps.

"Where are we going?" Theresa asked.

"We're going to try to find that store," I told her. "I'm sure they'll have a real phone there."

"Are we going the right way?"

"Yes," I said, even though I wasn't one hundred percent sure. But I was pretty sure.

We walked for a few minutes, Joe bounding happily along beside us.

Then I heard a car approach.

We quickly got off the road and back into the forest. As Joe ran past my legs, I scooped up the pug and carried him with me as we moved about fifty feet into the woods and ducked down out of sight.

This was the tricky part. We wanted somebody to help us, but we couldn't trust anybody. At the bare minimum, though, we needed to stay out of sight until we made sure it wasn't a green truck.

It was a black limousine.

It seemed pretty darn unlikely that anybody associated with the killers who were after us would be driving that kind of car, but I remained hidden.

The limousine was driving slowly. Almost too slowly. And though I couldn't yet see who was inside, I could tell the windows were down. On this hot, bug-laden road, there wouldn't be many vehicles driving slowly with their windows down unless they were looking and listening for somebody. Or their air conditioning was broken.

So the question was, was this somebody I wanted to find me?

Just as the car crossed in front of us, Joe barked.

I immediately slammed my hand over the dog's mouth.

The limousine stopped.

The door opened, and an unfamiliar woman got out. She was dressed entirely in red, and certainly didn't look like part of Ogre's team. But she also wasn't a police officer.

Who was she?

Maybe she was an innocent driver who just happened to be passing through, and the police recruited her to help out while they took Andrew to the hospital.

But why would anybody drive a limousine to a campground?

Of course, I didn't know that this road led only to Wreitzer Park. It could lead to a top secret government facility, for all I knew.

"Helen?" the woman called out in our direction. "Helen Mayhem?"

We stayed silent.

"I just heard from the police. Your husband is in stable condition. He's going to live."

She shut the door of the limousine and began to slowly walk toward the woods.

Could I trust her?

If I didn't trust somebody, the kids and I could end up walking around forever.

The woman paused at the edge of the woods, peering intently.

It didn't feel right.

She let out a whistle. "Here, doggie!" she called. "Here, doggie doggie! Good doggie! Come here!" She whistled again.

Joe struggled in my arms. Rotten disloyal pug.

"Heeeeeere doggie! I've got a treat for you!"

Joe was struggling too much. If I didn't let him go, he'd attract the woman's attention.

I released him and Joe ran toward the road. I placed a reassuring hand on Kyle's shoulder so he wouldn't call out.

Joe ran out of the woods and over to the woman. She knelt down, scratched his head, said a few baby-talk words I couldn't quite hear, and picked him up. She opened the limousine door and put him inside. Then she shut the door and looked back in our direction.

"Helen?" she asked again.

"Stay right where you are," I whispered to Kyle and Theresa. "If I tell you to run, run back into the woods, but don't move until I tell you, okay?"

My children nodded.

I stood up and slowly crawled away from them, not toward the road. Hopefully I'd make it a safe distance from them before the woman saw me, and there was enough cover that if she decided to whip out a gun and open fire, I'd be reasonably well-protected.

If she came after me...well, I'd beaten Ogre, and I could beat her.

I crawled for a couple of minutes, until I heard the limousine door open again. Then I stood up. "Hey!" I shouted.

The woman closed the door and turned back to look in my direction. "Helen?"

I waved at her. "Who are you?"

She walked toward the woods. "My name is Tracy. Man, am I glad to see you! I can't tell you what a messed-up day it's been!"

"Don't come any closer!" I warned.

She stopped. "That's fine, that's cool. I'm just here to take you into town. Where are your kids?"

"How did you get involved?"

"Just driving through, minding my own business."

"In a limo?"

She shrugged. "Picking up a client. One of those rich schmucks who go camping with satellite TV and an Internet connection."

"When will the cops be back?"

"No idea. They're pretty incompetent around these parts." She glanced at her watch. "Look, I know you're suspicious and stressed out and all that, but I'm getting eaten alive by these damn bugs and I'm gonna lose my job if I don't get you to the hospital and then pick up my client."

She seemed nice enough, but this didn't feel right. I've always had a really good internal bullshit detector (an absolute necessity when you're married to Andrew Mayhem) and though it wasn't sounding a red alert, it was definitely doing some beeping.

I couldn't trust this lady.

So now what?

I cautiously backed away, and then screamed in surprise and agony when something snapped shut over my ankle. As I fell to the ground, dropping the walkie-talkie, I saw it was a wolf trap.

Chapter Seventeen

Helen's Side

Though the rusty jaws of the wolf trap were flat rather than jagged, the pain was so intense it brought tears to my eyes.

I blinked the tears away, gripped the jaws of the trap tightly, and tried to wrench it open. The trap opened most of the way with a *creak* like teeth against a chalkboard...and then popped out of my grip and snapped shut over my foot again.

My reaction was not quiet.

The trap was attached to a chain wrapped around the base of a large tree, mostly hidden by leaves. Doing everything I could to force the excruciating pain out of my mind, I pried the trap open once again and withdrew my foot.

It snapped shut with a loud clang.

I didn't know if my foot was broken or not, but I did know I wouldn't be running on it anytime soon.

I stood up, bracing myself against the tree, and looked back at the road. The woman had entered the woods. She was holding a gun.

I wanted to call out to Theresa and Kyle, to scream at them not to move, but that would let the woman know where they were. I just had to pray they would stay put.

My breathing was so rapid I felt like I might hyperventilate. I quickly moved behind the tree, even though the pain shooting through my foot was worse than giving birth. It wasn't likely this tree could hide me for long, but it gave me a few seconds to figure out what to do.

Those few seconds passed without any grand revelation.

I could hear the woman approaching. She wasn't coming straight toward me, but rather to the side, probably trying to get a good shot without putting herself into harm's way. If I were lucky, maybe she'd step into a wolf trap of her own.

A flash of red clothing to my side.

I pulled out of the way just as a shot fired. It wasn't a loud gunshot, but more of a *swish*. Another shot, and a dart slammed into a tree next to me.

Still no brilliant plan of escape.

I sure as hell couldn't outrun her. The only thing I could do was try to climb the tree. Fast.

I reached up as high as I could, grabbed the lowest branch, and pulled myself up. I braced my feet against the trunk and "walked" up, which hurt worse than if Theresa and Kyle had been born simultaneously, but it didn't matter even if I was shattering every single bone in my leg. If I wanted to survive, I had to climb.

I screamed a lot, though.

I got my feet onto the lowest branch, and then pulled myself up onto the next one as quickly as I could. I could almost feel the adrenaline rushing through my veins as I climbed.

Swish!

A dart struck the branch inches from my right arm.

I continued climbing. I glanced down and saw the woman running toward the tree. There wasn't nearly enough branch cover, and I wasn't nearly high enough for her to miss unless she was a seriously crappy shot.

I pulled myself up to the next branch, and then my foot slipped. I hung there helplessly for a few seconds.

Swish!

The dart struck the bottom of my shoe. My uninjured foot, on the heel. It didn't break through to the skin.

I lifted my foot to the nearest branch, careful not to put my heel on it and push the dart in deeper. It remained wedged in my shoe. I continued to climb.

I heard the woman curse beneath me.

"Come down from there!" she shouted. "Don't be suicidal!"

She sounded frustrated. Maybe this meant she was out of darts.

I pulled myself up higher, scraping the hell out of my arm against a particularly sharp branch.

"Helen, this is ridiculous! You can't get away!"

I looked down. She was standing directly underneath me, probably thirty feet below. She cursed again, kicked the base of the tree, and then reached for the lowest branch.

Outclimbing her was going to be a bitch.

More than a bitch. Impossible. Even if I had a fire hose pumping adrenaline directly into my bloodstream, it wasn't gonna happen. I was still exhausted from my encounter with Ogre, and now every movement of my foot shot waves of pain all the way up my leg.

But I still kept climbing. I was about halfway up the tree, and it was starting to feel quite a bit less sturdy.

"What do you think you're going to do, Helen?" asked the woman.

She was only a couple of body-lengths behind me. "Climb the air after you've run out of tree? Come on down and let's settle this without me having to knock you to the ground."

I didn't answer her. I couldn't waste any energy by speaking.

The next branch I grabbed broke off in my hand and I momentarily lost my balance. I flailed, snatched another branch, and managed to prevent myself from saving the woman the effort of knocking me to the ground.

But what *was* I going to do when I got to the top of the tree?

I looked to the side. The next climbable tree was about ten feet away. There was no way I could jump straight across, but if I got in a really good leap I might be able to grab one of the lower branches as I fell.

I pulled myself up to the next branch. The woman continued climbing behind me, gaining quickly. She was directly beneath me, which suddenly gave me an idea.

I slammed my good foot against the branch. The dart in my shoe stayed in place. I slammed it once, twice, three more times, and then the dart came free.

The woman gasped.

I watched the dart fall.

It dropped past her arm and harmlessly hit the ground below.

The woman seemed more than a little upset by this near-miss, and began to climb after me with renewed energy. I reached for the next branch, which bent in half instead of supporting my weight. I grabbed another one, which also bent but not quite as badly.

I eased myself a couple of steps out onto the branch I was standing on. It wobbled beneath me. I swore I heard a cracking sound. If I was going to jump, I had to do it now, without thinking about it.

Of course, I'd *already* thought about it.

The branch beneath me snapped.

I let out a squeal as I hung there. I stretched out my good foot, trying to find something to stand on, but no branch was within reach.

As I struggled to pull myself up, the branch I was holding began to bow downward.

The woman reached out and grabbed for my bad foot. I swung it out of the way. She grabbed again, this time getting a handful of shoelace. She pulled my foot toward her then wrapped her fingers around my injured ankle and squeezed. I screamed, shut my eyes as if that would block out the pain, and lost my grip on the branch.

Freefall.

But only for a second. My butt smacked the next lower branch. I involuntarily leaned forward and continued falling, arms flailing wildly.

I struck the next lower branch with my shoulder.

The next with my knee.

The next one broke my fall. I scrambled to get myself oriented again, and then began to climb down the tree while the woman followed me, our chase now reversed.

Getting down required a lot less energy, and I tried to favor my good foot as I dropped to each lower branch. Again, the woman was gaining. Quickly.

When she was only one body-length away from me, she slammed her foot down on my hand. I let out yet another scream and fell. This time no branches broke my fall, and I plummeted about fifteen feet to the ground, landing once again on my ass.

I just lay there for a moment, dazed.

The woman hurriedly climbed down after me.

I tried to sit up but couldn't. I couldn't move.

Oh, God, what if I'd damaged my spinal column?

A lifetime of paralysis was a scary thought, although a useless concern, since if I *was* paralyzed I wouldn't be surviving the next couple of minutes.

The woman dropped to the ground at my feet. She wiped her hands off on her shirt and regarded me with disgust.

"I *hate* manual labor," she said. "It's a waste of my skills. When I have to chase you up and down a tree, all it does is make me think that instead of bringing you in alive like I'm supposed to, I should just kill you."

"Please," I said, hating myself for begging. "Just let—"

"Stop it. I don't want to hear it. If you think I feel any sympathy for a pathetic helpless female, you're wrong in a big way. Now, here's the question that determines whether you die quickly and painlessly, or slowly and miserably: Where are your kids?"

"Fuck you."

The woman sighed. "Okay, let me accentuate that last point. This is the question that also determines whether your *children* will die quickly and painlessly or slowly and miserably. Where are they?"

I wanted to spit in her face, but my projectile spitting skills weren't that advanced.

"Oooooh, steel resolve. I like that. I know they're around here somewhere. Probably close. You wouldn't leave them out in the middle of the woods by themselves. I sure hope you found them a good hiding spot. Maybe your dog will help me track them down, what do you think?"

Joe hadn't proven himself to be much of a tracker, but the woman was absolutely right. Theresa and Kyle were close. If she went out looking for them, she'd find them.

"Theresa! Kyle!" I screamed. "Run away! Run as fast as you can! Do it now!"

The woman spun around.

I grabbed the chain fastening the wolf trap to the tree and yanked on it as hard as I possibly could, nearly wrenching my arm out of its socket. As the woman turned back to face me, the wolf trap bashed into her chest, knocking her to the ground.

I forced myself to stand up, but immediately lost my balance and fell to my knees. I could see my children fleeing deeper into the woods. "Run!" I screamed again. Better to risk the booby traps than to have the woman catch them.

I raised the chain over my head and swung it again. This time it felt like my muscles were ripped right off the bone. The wolf trap flew toward the woman but she rolled out of the way and it struck the ground instead.

She got back up.

I scooted backward on my aching ass. I just had to stay alive long enough for my children to make it to safety.

The woman crouched down and pried open the jaws as far as they would go, setting the trap. Then she picked up the trap and walked toward me.

My hand brushed against something.

I threw the dart at her. It stuck in her leg.

She looked down at it in shock. Then she smiled. "What, you think there'd still be tranquilizer in there?" She plucked out the dart and tossed it aside.

Then she dropped to her knees.

Blinked a couple of times.

"You bitch," she said, tossing the wolf trap at me.

It landed between my legs, bounced once, and hit my upper thigh. The jolt in my heart was so great that for an instant I thought the trap had sprung.

The woman came toward me, still on her knees, arms extended, her eyes wide with fury even as her movements slowed.

I picked up the trap and slammed it against her face.

It sprung.

I turned away quickly, not wanting to see the results. Her body dropped onto mine, and I rolled her out of the way. I wiped her blood off my cheek, grateful it wasn't an eyeball or something like that. After all I'd been through, I didn't need to be wiping other people's eyeballs off my cheek.

Despite the gruesome sight right next to me, and despite the continued pain in my ankle and countless other parts of my body, I couldn't help but laugh. We now had a limo. We could get out of here. Drive away and find help. Rescue Andrew.

"Theresa! Kyle! It's safe now!" I shouted as loud as I could while being almost completely out of breath. "You can come back!"

I listened for their response.

Nothing.

"Theresa?"

I forced myself to stand up. My leg tried to buckle beneath me,

but I held steady. "Kyle? Honey? Come back!"
   Still nothing.
   Where were they?
   Oh, God, where were they?

Chapter Eighteen

I woke up, not even realizing I'd been unconscious.

The drug in the dart had obviously worn off because I could move again. That is, I could have moved again if my arms, legs, and torso hadn't been duct taped to a metal chair. They'd used a ridiculous amount...I practically looked like a duct tape mummy. My left hand had been bandaged up, which I hoped meant they planned to keep me alive for a while.

Roger and Samantha were similarly bound to my right, while Goblin was to my left. Goblin had received a black eye sometime between my loss of consciousness and now, and he looked scared and pitiful. He was the only one of the four prisoners who wasn't wearing a tight cloth gag.

We were in a large room with white tile floor and lockers lining the walls. There was a door on each side. The centerpiece was an operating table, surrounded by lights, and another table covered with what appeared to be a combination of medical equipment and home improvement supplies.

Witch was wiping down the operating table with bleach. Mr. Burke, Troll, and Medusa weren't around.

"Come on," Goblin pleaded. "You can't let them do this to me. I was a good boss, right? You were always my favorite. You know that."

Witch avoided looking at him and focused all of her attention on cleaning the operating table, looking sick to her stomach.

"Don't ignore me! It doesn't have to happen like this! You can just tell them I got free!"

"How?"

"I don't know. Make something up!"

"Yeah, right. Then I'll be on this table in your place."

"We can both go. Let's just leave. He'll do you next, you know. If he's disbanding our team there's no reason for him to keep you and Troll around. You'll die next. I promise you'll die next."

Witch shook her head. "No, I won't."

"You will, I swear. Witch, we're a team. You don't let this kind of shit happen to your teammates."

"We were never a team. You were the leader and we were the followers. You said that all the time." Her voice cracked. "And if you don't shut up I'll gag you."

Goblin lowered his head and began to weep softly.

A door behind me opened. Somebody walked into the room, and I felt a light slap on the back of my head. "Wakey-wakey!" said Troll, moving in front of me. He was soon followed by Mr. Burke. Troll was wearing green surgical scrubs, and Mr. Burke was in a white lab coat.

"Well, well, well," said Mr. Burke, rubbing his hands together. "Some lovely specimens we have here today. Who *shall* I work on first?"

"Do Goblin first," Troll suggested.

"Yes, that sounds like a fine idea. But let's take care of some other business before we get started." Mr. Burke looked at me, reached into the pocket of his lab coat, and removed a finger-sized object wrapped in tissue. "This was found in your pocket. Now, Andrew, do you really think proper storage of a severed digit includes keeping it in your filthy pocket?"

If I'd been able to speak, I probably would have said something along the lines of "Better than having it in Witch's mouth." Then again, I might not have.

Mr. Burke unwrapped my finger and shook his head sadly. "I don't know. Even with the amazing advances in laser surgery, I doubt this finger is in a sufficient state to be reattached. I think we're just going to have to give it the goldfish treatment."

He walked over and opened the door to my right, which led to a small bathroom. He held my finger over the toilet at chest-level, let it dangle for several seconds, then dropped it. It landed with a small splash.

"*Adios*, dear finger," said Mr. Burke. He flushed the toilet and watched happily. "Going...going..."

I wondered if this was payback for his being dunked in the toilet once too often by bullies in school.

"Going..." He frowned. "Aw, shit, it's still there. Fuckin' low-flow toilets." He flushed again. "Ah, there we go." He left the bathroom and shut the door behind him. "I'm afraid you won't be seeing your finger again."

I told him to *mmmphhh mmmmmmmphh* himself. I hadn't really counted on being able to save my finger anyway, but still, you never want to see your pinky get flushed by a madman.

"Let's hope it doesn't grow in the sewers like one of those alligators," said Troll. "It could come back for revenge."

"Indeed it could. We'll all just have to be careful."

Troll winked at me, and then ran his hand through Samantha's hair. He looked at Roger. "How did a babe like this ever end up with a dork like you?"

Roger's response was muffled but easy to translate and quite vulgar.

"Y'know," said Troll, still stroking her hair. "I wouldn't mind having some fun with this one myself."

Mr. Burke shook his head. "I want her alive when it's her turn on the table."

"I won't kill her."

"I've heard that before."

"No, really, I won't."

"I don't want any parts of her cut off, either."

"I won't."

Mr. Burke nodded. "All right. But if you betray my trust, the consequences will be severe."

"Am I allowed to break anything?"

Mr. Burke considered that. "Nothing vital. And do it in the other room. I don't want you distracting me."

"Ooooh, privacy. Even better. How about I drag her boyfriend in there with us to watch the show?"

"I think you're beginning to violate basic human decency, Troll," said Mr. Burke. "He needs to see what happens in here. Don't get greedy with your sadism."

Troll chuckled and walked behind Samantha's chair. As she screamed through her gag, he tilted her chair backward, and then dragged her across the floor in front of Roger and I, the chair making a horrible screeching sound as it scraped across the tile. Roger struggled violently but fruitlessly, shouting muffled curses the entire time.

Troll reached the door, opened it, and dragged Samantha into a dark room. When she was out of sight, he stepped back into the doorway and waved to us. "Have fun, everybody! I know I will."

Roger screamed in incoherent rage.

"What's that you're trying to say?" asked Troll. "She likes it rough? Thanks for the tip, buddy."

He closed the door.

"Don't let yourself be excessively stressed over this," Mr. Burke told Roger. "She'll still be at least seventy percent okay when he's done with her."

Roger gave him an absolutely chilling look.

Mr. Burke clapped his hands together. "So, let's get started, shall we? Goblin, are you prepared to pay the ultimate price for your failure?"

Goblin lifted his head. "Sir, *please*, I know I screwed up, but you have to give me another chance!"

"Oh, I *have* to, do I? Did you suddenly become the one in charge? Did I miss Promotion Day?"

"That's not what I meant, I just—"

"Then say what you mean, Goblin. Don't pretend I have any obligations to you or to anybody else."

"But I—"

"Stop speaking. Witch, gag him. No, on second thought, cut out his tongue. Use something inefficient to do it."

I didn't watch. But I had no way to cover my ears.

"Oh, now, that's cheating," said Mr. Burke, a couple of minutes later. He tapped me in the face with something sharp. "Open them."

I opened my eyes. He was holding a scalpel.

"Please keep your eyes open," he said, tapping the scalpel on each side of my nose. "You're being extremely rude, and I'd hate to have to slice off your eyelids."

I kept my eyes open as Mr. Burke and Witch lifted Goblin onto the operating table and quickly restrained him with a series of ten leather straps. He was making a hell of a lot more noise than when he'd been pleading for his life, but it was a much less coherent noise.

It was almost loud enough to block out the sound of Samantha screaming in the next room.

"Let's see, what's the best makeover for such a loyal employee?" Mr. Burke wondered aloud. "Oh, I know where to start. Witch, get me a left and right from locker 14."

Witch nodded sadly and went over to one of the lockers. She opened the door, revealing several sets of steel claws hanging inside. There was no palm to them, just five curved, pencil-sized blades welded together with a spike at the bottom. She took down a pair and placed them on the table.

"Ah, perfect," said Mr. Burke, putting on a pair of safety goggles. He picked up a handheld device with a circular blade. "Don't worry, Goblin. In just a moment you're going to look extremely cool."

He turned on the device. The motor hummed and the blade began to spin. Flesh, muscle, and bone separated with ease.

"We've got a bleeder," Mr. Burke announced, speaking loudly to be heard over the shrieks.

I was terrified that I was going to vomit under my gag and choke to death.

Mr. Burke replaced Goblin's hands with the claws, using the spikes to fix them in place.

I thought he might try to flush Goblin's original hands down the toilet, but Witch deposited them into a convenient waste receptacle.

I looked over at Roger. He was watching the door with Troll and Samantha behind it.

"Locker 27," Mr. Burke announced. "Let's give this gentleman a bionic eye."

"What color light?" Witch asked.

"How about...green?" Mr. Burke looked at me as if for my approval. Not knowing what else to do, I nodded. "Yes, green."

"Dark green or light green?"

"Dark green."

"Flashing?"

"Oh yes."

Witch opened another locker and removed a small metal circular object. She handed it to Mr. Burke, who flipped a switch on the side and held up the dark green flashing light for my approval. "Nice, isn't it?"

This time I didn't nod.

"Normally I'd remove the organic eye first," Mr. Burke explained. "But I think we'll skip that step and just wedge this one in as best we can."

Mr. Burke did so, though it took some effort. Goblin's screams and thrashing began to fade halfway through the process.

"Ah, yes, that looks great. I don't think you two can see it from where you're sitting, but trust me, that is a cyborg eye to die for. Now for the feet. Locker 2."

Mr. Burke went to work on Goblin's feet. This process didn't seem to be quite as easy as removing his hands, but it was completed in a quick and efficient manner.

Goblin's feet were replaced by wheels. He couldn't appreciate it, because by then he was dead.

Mr. Burke and Witch added some more enhancements. A row of copper spikes running down the sides of each leg. Bolts protruding from his neck, Frankenstein-style. The words "Cyber-Goblin 3000" burnt onto his chest.

"Excellent!" said Mr. Burke, wiping his hands off on a white towel. "Perhaps not one of my masterpieces, but a more than worthy addition to my collection."

Mr. Burke and Witch lifted Goblin's corpse onto a gurney. "Hose him off and prepare him for display," said Mr. Burke. Witch nodded and wheeled him past Roger and I and out the door behind us.

"See, I'm really not such a terrible individual," Mr. Burke told us. "It's not like I'm merely hacking up your bodies, mangling them for sport. When you were a child, wouldn't you have loved to look like the Cyber-Goblin 3000?"

He wiped off his face and neck, and then realized something. "Oh, I got so caught up in my work that I forgot to check in with Medusa. That's why it's so wonderful to be the boss: I'm allowed to screw up."

He picked up the walkie-talkie from the equipment table and pressed the button. "Medusa, come in."

He waited.

"Medusa?"

He set down the walkie-talkie and shrugged. "That's a promising sign. If she's shut off communications, your wife must be falling for her ruse. You know, Andrew, just between you and me, I could arrange to have her mouth replaced with a vacuum cleaner, if you know what

I mean." He gave an exaggerated wink.

Not being able to slam his face into one of Goblin's metal claws was an unbearably frustrating sensation.

"Actually, though, that's not in the plan. You see, I enjoy making my precious cyborgs, but right now we're just in the design phase. They look spectacular, but they don't really do anything because they're dead. But I've been wanting to test a special little something and this is the absolute perfect opportunity." He smiled. "I think you'll find it very, very interesting."

Chapter Nineteen

Mr. Burke brought the scalpel toward my face again, but this time he cut away the gag. "I probably should have untied that rather than cut it," he admitted. "I'm already over budget for the quarter. So what do you think so far? Be honest."

"I think you're a joke. What, you're making human action figures? How pathetically geeky is that?"

Mr. Burke chuckled. "Ah, Andrew, that comment would be much more devastating if you weren't so obviously terrified. You don't think I'm a joke. And I can tell that your friend here doesn't think I'm a joke. How about I check on his piece of tail?"

He walked over to the door Troll had taken Samantha through, opened it a crack, and peeked inside.

I wanted so badly to see Samantha's fist pop into view, punching Mr. Burke in the face, that for a moment I *did* see it.

But then I returned to reality. Mr. Burke closed the door and walked back over to us. "She's alive," he told Roger. "Though the word 'ouch' is probably appropriate. That Troll, he's a unique one, I'll give him that."

Witch returned to the room. "How does Goblin look?" Mr. Burke asked.

"Fine. Still leaking."

"Good, good." Mr. Burke picked up the walkie-talkie again and pressed the button. "Medusa?" Nothing. "Oh well." He set the walkie-talkie down then turned back to Witch. "Give Andrew here a quick shot so he doesn't wiggle so much."

Witch retrieved a hypodermic needle from the table. She jabbed it into my arm, and...

...I was suddenly on the operating table, strapped down by my wrists and ankles. A few tugs verified that I wasn't going anywhere. I could feel Goblin's blood, wet underneath me.

"Ah, good, you're awake already. That was quick." Mr. Burke held up a small camera, about two inches square and remarkably thin. "This is a wireless digital webcam," he explained. "The distance isn't great, not more than five hundred yards, but it'll do."

Witch turned on a blowtorch and began to heat up a thin strip of metal, also about two inches square with a pair of clamps on it.

"We'll get near-DVD quality picture and sound with this thing, so hopefully you'll provide sufficient entertainment value."

"I don't know what the hell you're babbling about," I said.

"You'll figure it out. What we've got for you, Andrew, is a very special serum. It's untested, so for all I know it could kill you the second we inject it, but let's hope it doesn't. That would be a waste. It's sort of a chemical cocktail, mixed with hallucinogens and paranoia enhancers...not the technical term...and all sorts of fascinating ingredients."

"I'm ready," said Witch, lifting the red-hot metal with a pair of tongs.

"Then I'm sure Andrew is, too. You may proceed."

Witch pressed the metal, clamps-side-up, right above my solar plexus. My entire body tightened up as I cried out, not even pretending I was going to deny Mr. Burke the pleasure of an extreme reaction. Witch pressed the metal more tightly against me and I could smell burning flesh and chest hair.

I strained against the leather straps, wanting desperately to rip the hot metal off my body.

"Ah, yes, that should stay in place quite nicely," said Mr. Burke, observing Witch's handiwork with satisfaction. "We'll just let it cool a bit and then attach the camera."

I found myself frantically blowing on the metal, as if that would help. Mr. Burke and Witch seemed to find this terribly amusing.

I could see that Roger was still struggling to break free of his chair, but making no progress.

"I think we're ready for the injection," said Mr. Burke. He leaned over me and spoke tenderly. "Now, this is going to hurt just a little bit, sort of like having your flesh shredded with a cheese grater from the inside and then microwaved. But don't worry, it's not addictive."

Witch patted my forearm to get a vein.

I struggled with every ounce of strength I could muster. In all of the times I'd been tied up or strapped down or otherwise prevented from enjoying freedom of movement, I'd never successfully managed to break free through the use of superhuman strength, and I was due. I visualized myself breaking free. I visualized Roger breaking free. I visualized Samantha breaking through the door and breaking us free. I visualized Kyle breaking through the ceiling in a superhero cape and breaking us free.

I remained strapped to the bloody operating table.

Witch held up the hypodermic needle, squeezing some liquid out to avoid injecting an air bubble into my bloodstream. She brought it down slowly toward my arm.

I started to become concerned that my final thought in this world might be something stupid like my seven year-old son breaking through a ceiling in a superhero cape, but I couldn't force myself to think of anything else.

Witch slid the needle into my skin.

A warm, almost soothing feeling began to flow through my arm.

Followed immediately by the most devastating pain I'd ever felt in my life. A dozen times worse than, say, chopping off my finger or having a red-hot piece of metal pressed against my chest.

I screamed and screamed and screamed.

Then, for a change of pace, I shrieked and shrieked and shrieked.

I may have said "Ow!"

It really, really hurt.

"My, my, listen to Andrew scream," said Mr. Burke. His chuckle echoed throughout the room.

It didn't *really* echo, did it?

Yes, it did. In fact, it was still echoing. And getting louder. I heard it in stereo.

Mr. Burke smiled, revealing oversized teeth.

I looked at my straps and gasped in horror. They'd transformed into...well, they were still leather straps, but they were unexplainably *scary* leather straps.

"Is it working, Andrew?" asked Mr. Burke, his voice dropping an octave or two. "How do you feel?"

"I hurt."

"How does your mind feel?"

"I don't know. I think it hurts."

Mr. Burke held up his hand in front of me. "How many fingers am I holding up?"

"Three," I said. Suddenly that seemed amazingly funny. Three fingers! He was holding up three fingers! Right in front of my face! I giggled.

Giggling was so much more fun than screaming. But screaming had its positive aspects, too, like giving your lungs a workout and keeping them healthy, and alerting people to your presence who might otherwise ignore you, and...

I giggled some more.

I raised my back as much as I could. "I think something is swimming in Goblin's blood," I informed Mr. Burke.

"And what do you think that might be?" he asked.

"I dunno. You tell me." I giggled at my joke. "I think it's a little man swimming in there. A tiny little man swimming in Goblin's blood. I hope he doesn't pee in it."

"I hope he doesn't either," said Mr. Burke, still smiling at me with those oversized, way-too-white teeth.

"You've got funky teeth," I told him. "Pull them out for me."

"I'm afraid I can't do that."

"Oh. Bummer."

I looked over at Roger, who looked hilariously miserable. He almost looked like he was going to cry. And he was a grown man!

I laughed at him.

I suddenly realized that I didn't hurt anymore. And that there were now several tiny little men swimming in Goblin's blood. One of them was doing the breaststroke.

"You know," I told Mr. Burke, "it takes a lot of work to kill a man with paper cuts, but I'm patient."

Mr. Burke kept smiling. All of his face was gone except for his teeth.

"You know what?" I asked.

"What?"

"That's what." I frowned. "That wasn't funny. You know what?"

"What?"

"That's what." I laughed hysterically, and then I slammed myself against the table a couple of times to crush the millions of tiny little men swimming in Goblin's blood.

"Tell me, Andrew, are you afraid of demons?"

"Dee-mons! Dee-mons!"

"There are demons everywhere, you know."

"Spooky scary demons!"

"There's one in this room."

"Creepy crawly demons!"

"You hate demons."

I nodded. "Demons suck."

"Indeed they do."

"Yanking off a hangnail with a staple remover is overrated."

"Indeed it is."

"Doesn't it hurt just having teeth for a face? What if you have to blow your nose? I just don't understand how it works, I'm sorry."

"Look over there," said Mr. Burke, pointing. "Do you see the demon?"

I did indeed. It was a female demon, wearing a white lab coat spattered with blood. She was one serious babe, even though she had red scaly flesh and eyes that literally smoldered.

It was clearly a succubus. Or was it an incubus? I always got those two confused. It was a continual source of shame and embarrassment.

The demon hissed at me. I hissed back.

"You want to kill it, don't you?"

"Nah."

"Andrew, it's a demon. Aren't you the mighty demon slayer?"

"What kind of dumb shit are you talking about? Demon slayer, hemon slayer. I need to slay more hemons. What's a hemon? I'm hungry."

"The demon is looking into your soul, Andrew."

My God. He was right. The demon *was* staring right into my soul. It was learning my secrets, laughing at them, mocking them, sharing them with its demon brethren. The demon's evil was exploring inside me, wriggling around like worms, devouring its way into my heart.

"Make it stop," I begged.

"Only you can make it stop."

"It's *scaring* me!"

"Scare it back."

"It's going to eat me! Don't let it eat me!"

"You're being tested, Andrew. You can pass the test. You must learn to hate the demon, not fear it."

"I hate how scary it is!"

"Hate. Hate is the key. Control your hate. Control your rage. Don't let the demons win. Can you do that? Can you truly, deeply hate?"

"I...I think so."

"That's not good enough."

"Yes, I can."

"There are demons in the woods, Andrew. They're lost demons trying to find their way back home. Three of them. A mother and two children. Can you hate them?"

"Yes."

"Can you kill them?"

"Yes."

"I'm going to give you a knife. Can you slam it into the bodies of those foul creatures, no matter how much they scream, no matter what tricks they try to play on you? Because demons will lie to you. They'll change form. They'll pretend they love you. Can you kill them?"

"Yes."

"Then I shall release you."

I could feel the hatred flowing through me, just as the pain had flowed through me before. The hatred felt good.

Really, really good.

❦

I rode in a chariot of gold, pulled by two fire-breathing steeds that were the most beautiful animals I'd ever seen in my life, even when they started ripping out chunks of each other's flesh.

The world was cast into darkness, but the sun burned my eyes.

I smiled at my hatred. At my rage. That's what kept me strong. Demons were weak. Their compassion was their weakness, and I'd exploit that until their severed heads rested at my feet. Granted, the knife I'd been given really didn't seem sufficient for a demonic decapitation, but I'd worry about that when the time came.

The chariot stopped.

"You must go now," Mr. Burke said. "You must fulfill your destiny."

"Will I ever see you again?"

"Yes. I will give you this beacon." Mr. Burke extended a sparkling silver object toward me. He affixed it to the metal plate burned into my chest, my mark of honor. "This will let us find you, and bring you home."

"Will you be watching over me?"

"I won't, but your guardian angel will. I'll watch the recording after you're back all safe and sound."

"Thank you." I hugged him as if he were my father.

Then I began on my journey.

I wandered for days. No, not days, but months. Years. For years I wandered the dirt path, fearful of the horrific noises emanating from the forest on each side but not letting my fear show.

I cradled my precious knife in my hands.

I realized I hadn't eaten or slept in years. That was kind of weird.

To help the months pass, I decided to make up a song. The Demon Song.

I am the demon hunter named Andrew.

Whose exploits will...

What rhymed with "Andrew?"

Andrew, Bandrew, Candrew, Dandrew...

I am the demon hunter named Mayhem.

Whose exploits will...

Damn.

Demons, demons, time to die.

For I will poke you in the eye.

And then you shall begin to cry.

As I sing your fatal lullaby.

I grinned at my own cleverness.

"Daddy!"

I spun around. A horrid creature emerged from the woods, its scaly skin as red as Red Vines brand original licorice twists.

The little girl demon.

The creature was so repulsive, so gag-inducing, I wanted to fling my knife at it and end its vile life right now.

But I wasn't that good at knife throwing, and I didn't want to lose my weapon. Anyway, demons were tricky creatures, and so I had to be careful.

It was running toward me.

"Daddy! Daddy!" it repeated.

This demon looked somehow familiar...

I hated it.

I wanted to rip its head off of its tiny shoulders.

It was moving quickly.

Don't fear it, don't fear it, don't fear it.

No demon could harm me.

Nothing could harm me.

A tree looked like it was eating somebody, but it may also have been bathing them.

I held my ground as the demon rushed at me.

Yes, I knew this one! Its name was Theresa!

Dumb name for a demon.

The demon stopped a few feet away from me. It bit its scaly lip as if unsure about something.

"Daddy? Are you okay?"

I knew I'd be a lot better if this piece of crap demon stopped calling me "Daddy." I wasn't the parent of any hellspawn.

The demon backed away.

Did it really believe I was its father?

It couldn't possibly. But its tone of voice was so convincing.

Demons were tricky creatures.

I could be tricky, too.

"I'm fine," I said, in my most soothing voice as I hid the knife behind my back. "Come here. Come to Daddy."

The demon walked toward me.

Slowly, untrusting.

I had to bite my own lip to keep from laughing.

"Daddy, what's wrong?"

"Nothing's wrong, Theresa."

"Did they hurt you?"

I nodded. "They hurt Daddy bad. He needs you to comfort him. That will make everything okay."

The demon walked up to me and wrapped its filthy arms around me. I wanted to gag.

I pushed the monster away.

"Daddy...?"

I slammed the knife into it, laughing as its warm blood spattered against my bare chest.

Chapter Twenty

Helen's Side

Where could they be?

"Theresa!" I shouted, loud enough that it made my throat burn. "Kyle! Where are you?"

I had horrible visions of my children caught in wolf traps, impaled by spears, dangling from meat hooks, and worse. Much worse. Grisly supernatural deaths at the hands of ghouls and ogres. Pretty much any tragic fate that could befall my children, possible or impossible, flashed across my mind as I wandered through the woods.

I couldn't go through all this only to lose them now. It just couldn't happen. I cried out for them once more, not caring if I was alerting more killers to my presence.

Then I remembered the limousine.

I limped toward the road, drenched with sweat, each step feeling like a great white shark was chomping on my ankle. I fell twice, but I doubted I could make even this much progress if I'd broken anything, so as far as I could tell my ankle was seriously messed up but still in one piece.

I fell again when I reached the dirt road. I knew I had to be a sorry sight. A pregnant woman who'd been beaten half to death. It would be a miracle if I hadn't lost the—

NO NO NO NO NO!!!

The baby was fine! I was absolutely positive that the baby was one hundred percent completely perfectly fine.

I wept for it anyway.

I got up and staggered toward the limousine. I opened the driver's side door and Joe happily jumped up onto the seat. He wasn't exactly my favorite canine at the moment, but it's hard to stay mad at a pug.

Kyle sat in the front seat.

"Kyle! Oh, thank heavens, sweetie!" I climbed into the car and reached for him, giving him a smothering hug that he returned. "I was so worried about you!"

My son buried his face against my belly and cried.

But my relief was short-lived. "Where's Theresa?" I asked.

"I don't know," said Kyle, his face still pressed against my belly.

I pushed him back and looked him in the eye. "Did you see her?"

"She brought me here. She told me to stay in the car. She said she was going to help you."

"Are you sure? I didn't see her out there. She didn't answer me. What exactly did she say?"

"I don't know."

"Kyle, *think*. Where's your sister? Did she say she was going to *help*, or to *get* help?"

"I don't know!"

I closed my eyes, took a few deep breaths to calm myself, and then opened them. "It's okay, we'll find her. Stay in the car and see if you can find a phone or walkie-talkie or anything like that. If you find a gun, let me know, but don't touch it."

Kyle nodded.

"I'll be back in five minutes. Promise me you'll stay in the car."

"I will."

"Good." I gave him another hug and a kiss on the cheek.

There was a plastic bottle of water in the cup holder with pink lipstick smears on the rim. I grabbed it, gulped down half of the contents, and gave the bottle to Kyle. "I love you, honey."

"I love you too."

"It'll all be fine."

I returned to the woods and called out Theresa's name again and again. Where could she have gone? I couldn't imagine she would have taken the time to get her brother to safety but then run off in a blind panic.

I searched for the full five minutes, my foot hurting worse with each passing minute, and finally returned to the limousine. Kyle handed me the bottled water as I got in on the driver's side and I quickly drank the rest of it.

"Did you find anything?" I asked him.

Kyle had a red purse pressed between his knees and he'd poured the contents out onto his lap. "A phone. But it didn't work."

I took the cell phone from him and dialed. No signal.

"Did you find anything else?"

"These," he said, holding up a strip of condoms.

"Let's put those back in the purse," I said, taking them from him. "And these, too." I replaced the tampons. Joe was on the floor, chewing on a tampon like a bone, so I took it from him and put it in the purse as well.

"Can I have a piece of gum?" Kyle asked.

"Yes, you can have the whole pack."

Kyle looked at the gum sadly. "I'll give Theresa the rest when we find her."

I shut the limo door. The keys were still in the ignition, so I started the motor. "I need you to watch out the window and look for your sister."

"Which way do you think she went?"

"I don't know, honey. But we're going to be going really fast, so watch as closely as you can."

I applied the gas and we sped down the road. I slowed down when we went around corners, just in case my daughter was wandering in the middle of the road, but apart from that I floored the gas.

"Try to dial 911 again," I said, handing Kyle the phone. "Is there a signal?"

He shook his head. "No."

"Just keep trying."

We continued to race along the dirt road.

"I'd like a piece of that gum," I told Kyle. He unwrapped a piece and I popped the strawberry gum into my mouth. I'd never been much of a gum or candy person, but this tasted absolutely delicious. I even blew a bubble.

Two minutes later, we still couldn't get a signal.

"Do you think Theresa walked this far?" Kyle asked.

"No, I'm sure she didn't, but I just want to find a phone signal so we can call for help. I think we're getting close to the freeway, and we'll definitely be able to get a signal there."

Kyle nodded and pressed redial again.

"It's working!" he shouted. "It's working!"

I grabbed the phone from him and pressed it tightly to my ear. A ring on the other end. And then a cheerful female voice: "911 emergency."

I applied the brakes, harder than I'd intended. "Oh, thank God, my name is Helen Mayhem and there's been an accident and my family has been very badly injured!"

"Ma'am, please give me your location."

I gave her the directions as best I could. I didn't want to tell her about the killers, for fear that she wouldn't believe my story, but at the same time I couldn't risk letting the police come in unprepared.

So I told her everything.

She seemed to believe me.

I turned the limousine around (not an easy process) and then sped back the way we came. I lost the signal moments after that. With renewed energy, I drove off to find my family.

❧ ❧

I found them.

I was so astonished at my good fortune that I nearly squealed with delight, and I'm not a squealer. Standing there, right in the middle of the road up ahead, were Andrew and Theresa, locked in a tight hug. I could see he was holding a knife. Hopefully a bloody knife that had slit the throats of the bastards who attacked us.

"It's them!" I squealed, proving that I am a squealer in the right circumstances. "It's Theresa and Daddy!"

They were alive!

They were safe!

I felt a sudden pang of concern as I realized Roger and Samantha were nowhere around, but I was overjoyed to see my husband and my daughter were both alive.

And then Andrew pushed Theresa away and stabbed her in the chest.

I immediately knew I hadn't really seen that. Maybe I was so overwhelmed with elation I wasn't seeing straight, or maybe this whole experience had finally driven me to insanity, but I knew for certain I hadn't just seen Andrew stab our daughter.

And I didn't see him laugh as she fell to the ground.

And I didn't see him crouch down over her body and raise the knife.

"*Mommy!*" Kyle's shriek was so loud it snapped me out of my state of disbelief and made me realize what I was seeing was completely real.

Better to have gone insane.

I floored the gas pedal and the limousine rocketed forward. Andrew looked up at the car, still holding the knife in the air. I slammed on the brakes right before I reached him.

"Stay in the car!" I wailed at Kyle as I threw open the door and got out. "Andrew! Stop!"

He looked at me, confused. His eyes were wild and unfocused.

Theresa was bleeding badly, gasping for breath, and clawing at her wound.

"You don't scare me," Andrew said.

I walked toward him, slowly, carefully, trying not to set him off. If he chose to plunge the knife into Theresa again, I wouldn't be able to stop him.

"Andrew, please, look at me."

He grinned. "I *am* looking at you! What, you got problems with those demon eyes of yours? Maybe you should pop 'em out and put in a new pair!" He gestured at Theresa with the knife. "Wanna try hers?"

I spoke slowly, calmly. "Please, Andrew, you don't want to hurt your daughter."

"I don't have a daughter. I'm a freeeeeeee demon slayer!" He let out a joyous whoop.

What the hell had they done to him?

"Mommy..." said Theresa, weakly, reaching her arm out toward me.

"Please, let me take her," I said. "She'll bleed to death."

Andrew ran his index finger across the stab wound and held it up, looking at it closely. "It looks like oil. You demons bleed black oil. That must be why you live in fire."

"She's not a demon. She's your daughter."

"She's *not* my daughter!" Andrew shouted. "She's a disgusting, rotting creature! And I'm not scared of you!"

But he was. His fear was obvious. Was he really seeing demons?

I took a step forward. "That's right, she is a demon. And if you touch her, I'll destroy you."

Andrew snorted. "I'm not scared."

"*GET THE FUCK AWAY FROM MY DAUGHTER OR I'LL DRAG YOU INTO THE PITS OF HELL!*" I screamed.

Andrew cried out in fear and scrambled away from her. I could now see he had something that looked like a camera attached to his chest.

I strode forward and raised my arms to become more intimidating. "*YOU'LL BURN WITH US!*"

"No!" Andrew got to his feet. "I'll kill all of you!"

He rushed at me with the knife.

I moved out of the way, but then I twisted my foot and fell to the ground.

Theresa's breathing was rapid and frantic.

I got up as quickly as I could, just in time for Andrew to thrust the knife at me. It tore across my side, cutting deep.

I punched Andrew in the face.

He put his hand to his cheek and stumbled away. "Oh, shit, it burns!"

I let out my best approximation of a demonic roar. Under any other circumstances I would have felt completely ridiculous, but now, in the moment, I felt like I truly *was* a demon.

"I'll eat you alive!" I screamed.

Andrew lunged at me with the knife but missed.

I heard the car door open behind me.

"Daddy, stop!" Kyle screamed.

"Kyle, get back in the car!"

"Daddy, don't hurt her!"

Andrew swung at me again. The tip of the blade sliced across my chest, but it was just a scratch.

"Kyle, breathe fire!" I shouted. "Breathe fire on him! Burn him! Burn his eyes out!"

Andrew raised his arm to shield his eyes.

I punched him in the stomach. He doubled over and staggered away, groaning. The knife fell out of his hand and he reached down to pick it up.

I rushed for the weapon, and our hands met upon its handle. We struggled for a moment, but it was quickly clear he was going to win.

Our gazes locked. As I lost my grip on the knife, I stared into his eyes, trying to see if there was any hint of recognition, anything I could use to bring my husband back to reality.

Nothing. Just pure fear.

I glanced down. It *was* a camera mounted on his chest. I wrapped my fingers around it and pulled as hard as I could.

Andrew cried out as the metal plate affixing the camera to his chest started to tear free. The flesh underneath was red and blistered and bloody and I realized with horror that the plate had been burnt onto him.

He slapped me, hard, but I didn't let go.

The camera ripped free, taking pieces of skin with it.

Andrew howled with pain and pressed his hand to the wound. "My beacon!" he shouted.

I flung the camera toward the woods as hard as I could. It smacked into a tree and fell to the ground.

Andrew got to his feet, whimpering. "Where is it? What did you do with it?"

"Andrew, please! You're not in your right mind! They did something to you!"

"Where's my beacon?"

"Your name is Andrew Mayhem. Andrew Mayhem! It's a goofy name, but it's yours!"

"I *know* what my fucking name is!"

"And I'm Helen Mayhem. I'm your wife."

"I don't have a wife."

"And Theresa is your daughter. Kyle is your son."

"Shut up!"

"Andrew, I love you!" I said, somehow managing to stand back up. "We all love you!"

Andrew slammed his hands over his ears. "*Shut up!*"

"Andrew, please, come back to us!"

It was working. I could feel it working.

"*I said shut up!*"

I stepped toward him. My leg wobbled and I nearly lost my balance, but I did it.

"This isn't you."

"You don't know who I am!"

"I know exactly who you are. You're the man I married."

Andrew stared at me.

Was that a flash of recognition in his eyes?

A flash of love?

"Helen...?" he asked.

"Yes, it's me!"

His voice cracked. "Helen...what have I done?"

Chapter Twenty-One

"It wasn't your fault," it said. "They did something to you."

I nodded. "Yes, they did something to me."

Blood was gushing from where the demon had ripped off my beacon. It was pouring out like a waterfall. I didn't even know I *had* that much blood, but yet it gushed out, quickly soaking into the ground as it hit.

The larger demon took another step toward me. I forced myself not to cry out in fear or disgust. I had no idea what trick this creature was trying to play by insisting it was my wife...my *wife*, if such a revolting thing could even be imagined...but maybe if I played along I could defeat it.

"Where are Roger and Samantha?" the demon asked.

I shrugged.

"Are they alive?"

Yes? No? What was the best answer? Did this demon fear them? Did this demon need them?

"I don't know," I said.

The demon stepped away from me. Its scaly, slimy skin glistened in the sunlight. "I'm taking Theresa," it said.

It crouched down next to the fallen demon. I couldn't let it do this. I'd be punished if I didn't slay them. I had to kill them as quickly as possible.

"I'm going to send help for you," the demon said. "Everything will be okay, I promise."

The demon scooped up the smaller creature in its wretched arms.

Blood continued to pour from my chest. And then it squirted from my eye. I wasn't sure how I could see blood squirting out of my eye, but I could. Suddenly it was squirting out of both eyes.

"Stop it!" I demanded, rubbing at my eyes to block the flow. "I need that blood in me!"

The blood that had soaked into the ground began to bubble to the surface, quickly rising over my shoes.

The demon had cursed me.

I saw faces in the blood. Screaming faces. Laughing faces. Crying faces. All of them looking at me.

I turned and ran.

I didn't care if I'd be punished. I didn't care if the demons got away. I just had to escape from this place, get out of here before I drowned in my own blood and the faces sunk their fangs into me.

I ran into the forest. Sap oozed from the trees, trapping birds and squirrels and other forest animals within. Razor blades flowed in the sap, slicing the poor things without mercy.

I smacked into a tree, knocking my face off. It hit the ground, face-down. I continued running, leaving it behind.

Trees reached for me with their branches, ripping off my arms and legs, which were quickly replaced with new arms and legs for the trees to rip off. I'd never realized I had so many arms and legs.

I wished my chest would quit bleeding. This was starting to get ridiculous.

As I ran, I glanced behind me (without turning my head, which was odd) and saw a giant pile of my twitching arms and legs. I could also see a tongue flapping around in there, even though my own tongue was clearly still in my...oh, nope, wait, it was gone.

I ran out into a dirt clearing. An infinite clearing, where the trees couldn't detach any more of my limbs.

In fact, the clearing was kind of boring.

I twiddled my thumbs.

I twiddled my tongues, since I now seemed to have two.

That demon *had* looked kind of familiar, now that I thought about it. Maybe I'd tried to slay her in some other plane of existence. Maybe we'd dated. It seemed unlikely that I'd ever dated a demon, but I'd done some experimenting in college.

I heard a sound like a squeaky faucet handle turning, and the blood flow from my chest grew weaker and weaker until it stopped altogether. With a sound like a zipper closing, the wound healed back up, leaving only a scar that read "Do Not Pry Open."

The ground began to rumble.

Earthquake!

Or a tornado with ground-rumbling properties!

Tornado with ground-rumbling properties. That was just silly. I laughed at my own foolishness, which was difficult with seventeen or eighteen tongues in my mouth.

And my severed pinky. I wondered how that got in there.

Something was emerging from the ground in front of me. I hoped it was a bag of gold instead of a zombie.

The object broke free to the surface.

It was a tombstone. The inscription read "Graverob *This*, Asshole."

Another tombstone burst out of the ground: "R.I.P. Andrew Mayhem." Then another: "R.I.P. Helen Mayhem." Theresa and Kyle Mayhem followed.

Now hundreds of tombstones were bursting through the ground. One emerged directly underneath my feet, knocking me to the ground. As I fell I hit my head on a tombstone, knocking off the top half of my skull.

I lost consciousness for a few years.

When I recovered, I yanked off my new beard and realized I was surrounded by millions of tombstones. They were so close together that the people had to be buried standing up, or several bodies deep. Or else they were really tiny people.

I bellowed in terror, just for the hell of it.

Goblin made his way through the tombstones. My arch-nemesis was looking bad, his face a patchwork of scars and gashes, but I had to admit his cyborg makeover did look pretty cool.

"Andrew," he said, nodding politely.

"Goblin," I said, returning his nod.

"Why aren't you digging?" he asked.

I shrugged. "Dunno."

"Don't you know where you are?"

I looked around without moving my head. The iron gates read "Sanity Cemetery." "I'm in Sanity Cemetery," I replied. "Duh."

"Your sanity is buried here, Andrew," Goblin informed me.

"I'm insane?"

"Yes."

"That sucks."

"Surely you don't think all of this is real, do you?"

One of my tongues popped out of my mouth and oozed along the ground like a speedy slug. "Dunno."

"You must dig," Goblin said. He peeled off one of his scars like a sticker. "Dig deep."

"With what?"

Goblin pointed to my right arm. It had become a shovel.

"Ah, thanks," I said.

"Dig."

Okay, I'd dig. Digging was fun.

A tombstone in front of me read "Casket For Sale (Only Used Once). Serious Inquiries Only, Please." There was a glowing red X in the dirt in front of it. I wondered if this could be some sort of sign.

I began to dig. It wasn't easy, because when you're digging with a regular shovel you use your feet to slam it into the ground, but I couldn't do that because the shovel was my arm, and so it was pretty awkward at first and it was kind of hurting my back, not to mention the whole weirdness factor of having my own arm be a shovel, I mean, the tongues were weird, too, but at least they were just multiples of a standard body part, while a shovel was a completely foreign appendage to the human body.

At least the ground was soft.

"*Gonna dig that grave, gonna dig it deep*," I sang, as a chorus of souls in torment accompanied me. "*Gonna dig my sanity right out of the dirt.*"

"*He's gonna dig his sanity right out of the dirt!*" sang the tormented souls.

Helen Mayhem. Why did that name sound so familiar?

Oh, right. Because she had the same last name as me.

I dug and dug and dug. Worms squirmed out of the sides of the hole and recited non-rhyming poetry to me.

Theresa Mayhem sounded familiar, too.

Oh, right. The last name thing again.

The hole was now well over six feet deep. That damn tombstone better not have been lying about the casket for sale.

Kyle Mayhem. That name also rang a bell. I couldn't quite put my finger on why it rang that bell, or what particular bell it rang, but...

Was he my son?

My arm-shovel struck casket.

I crouched down and brushed the dirt away. It was a pretty nice casket. I wondered why somebody would sell it.

I threw open the lid.

My brain was inside.

I picked it up, being careful to use both hands so I didn't drop it. It was lighter than I expected.

Helen. Theresa. Kyle.

Where was I supposed to put this brain? I did a quick check and saw that the top of my skull was still missing. "Hey, Goblin, watch this!" I said, tossing my brain up into the air as high as I could.

Helen in my arms, the baby in her womb...

My brain sailed back down to earth. I positioned my skull just right.

Helen almost breaking every bone in my hand during labor with Theresa...

Almost there...almost there...

Kyle, the most beautiful baby ever born in the entire world, even with that gook all over him...

Perfect catch!

"I'm sane!" I cried out. "In your face, multiple tongues!"

I began kicking tombstones out of the way as I did my victory lap. They scattered to the wind like playing cards. "Goooooooo Team Mayhem! Woo-hoo!"

I smacked into a tree.

Then I threw up.

I tried to spit the extra tongues out of my mouth, but they weren't there.

My finger hurt. At least the stump did.

I braced myself against the tree and vomited again. What a horrible, horrible nightmare, but it was already starting to fade...

No, it wasn't. Nothing was fading but the visions.

I wasn't a demon slayer. I was a husband and a father and a best friend.

And a madman.

I'd tried to kill Helen.

I'd stabbed Theresa.

The reality of the situation hit me with such force that for several long moments I could do nothing but stand there, gasping for breath.

One of the tombstones fluttered past my ear and faded away.

I bent over, but there was nothing left to vomit. I dry heaved a few times, and then wiped off my mouth and desperately tried to figure out what to do.

It didn't take long to come up with the answer. Of course, it was a vague answer, not particularly helpful, and without a plan of action attached to it, but at least I knew I had to get back to my family and get them to safety.

Chapter Twenty-Two

I hadn't gone far into the woods, and as I emerged onto the road Helen had just finished getting Theresa into the limousine. She looked over at me. It was going to take crates of chocolate, truckloads of roses, and the combined efforts of Hallmark's finest to get me out of this one.

"I'm fine now," I said, keeping my distance. "I swear I'm fine now."

"How do I know that?"

"Well...you won't hear me babbling about being a demon slayer anymore."

Helen didn't respond.

"They gave me some weird drug," I said. "I don't know what it was, but they injected me with it and it turned me into a...it turned me into somebody who would do what I did. But it wasn't me."

"I know," Helen said.

"Is there a gun in the car?" I asked. "Duct tape, maybe? Some way for you to be sure I won't hurt you? I won't, I swear I won't, but I don't expect you to believe me. I could ride in the trunk."

"There's duct tape."

"How's Theresa?"

"You hurt her bad."

I forced myself to fight back tears. "She'll be okay, right?"

"I have to get her medical attention as soon as possible. I've patched her up with what I could find but she lost a lot of blood. Andrew, I have to go."

"No! I need to go with you! Helen, I know you don't trust me and I don't expect you to, but Roger and Samantha are still in serious danger, and we have to save them! And the rest of the maniacs could be here any—"

Witch came around the corner.

She was walking, holding a revolver, and looked completely beat.

"Don't move," she said, pointing the gun at me as she walked. "Just stay where you are."

I raised my hands in the air. Helen looked uncertain about whether she should take the risk of trying to get into the limousine.

Witch stopped about ten feet away from us. "This is all bullshit," she said, her voice a monotone. "We're not getting out of this one, I can feel it. I had to help kill a man who didn't even know I loved him. I just don't care anymore." She shook her head sadly. "All of you can run. Maybe you'll get away, maybe you won't, but either way, it's not my problem."

She turned the revolver away from me and put the barrel in her mouth. Then she closed her eyes and pulled the trigger.

Nothing happened.

She pulled the trigger a couple more times, removed the barrel from her mouth, and opened her eyes. "Well," she said. "This is awkward."

"Do you, uh, want to borrow a knife?" I asked.

Witch shook her head.

"I could give you directions to a spiked pit. That would do the trick."

"Nah, I'm just going to head back to my truck, I guess. If they catch me, they catch me." She sighed, and then turned around and started walking back the way she came.

I was pretty sure she wouldn't let us use her as a hostage again, so I returned my attention to Helen. "We have to get out of here," I said. "Roger and Samantha could still be alive."

Helen nodded. "You can ride with us. Theresa and Kyle will be in the back. You know that if you make a move for them, I'll have to kill you."

"I understand."

"I mean it."

"I believe you," I said, hurrying over. "I'll drive. You get in the back with the kids."

Moments later I was behind the wheel and we sped off, only to slow down again. Witch was in the middle of the road, walking slowly.

I honked. She didn't seem to even hear it.

I wasn't sure what to do here. Should I just run her over? That seemed kind of extreme, considering that she was basically harmless at this point and her body would most likely get wedged underneath the limousine and delay our escape.

I honked again.

She moved slightly to the left, giving me just enough room to get around her. I floored the gas pedal and we sped off.

"Andrew, your finger!" Helen exclaimed, looking at me from the back of the limo.

"Yeah, it got flushed," I said. "What happened to your foot?"

"Wolf trap. What happened to your face?"

"Flying debris from the camper when it exploded, a few thousand punches, I smacked into a couple of trees..." I glanced up at the rear-view mirror and noticed Kyle watching me carefully. "Kyle, I'm really sorry about this," I said. "They forced Daddy to take medicine that screwed with his brain, but I would never, ever hurt you."

"You hurt Theresa," he said in a quiet voice.

"I know, but it wasn't really me. It was the bad men."

Kyle turned away and looked out the window.

"How's Theresa doing?" I asked.

"She's unconscious."

"Is there a cell phone back there? Maybe we can get a signal now."

Helen brightened just a bit. "I did! The police are on their way!"

An explosion nearly sent the limo careening off the road. I quickly regained control of the vehicle and kept up the rapid speed as I glanced over at the source of the explosion. Something huge had blown up in the woods.

"What was that?" Helen asked, moving to the other side of the limo to peer out the window.

"I'm guessing it was their lab," I said, feeling utterly sick to my stomach. That is, even more utterly sick to my stomach than I was already feeling. "They must know that the cops are on their way. They're probably getting out and trying to cut down on the evidence."

"Do you think Roger and Samantha were...?"

"They're fine. They have to be fine." Unless Mr. Burke and Troll had gone suicidal like Witch, they probably weren't in the lab when it exploded. And they might have brought along Roger and Samantha, if only as hostages.

I'd gone through too much on this crappy vacation to lose my best friend. It was possible I'd never be able to reconcile with my family, but at least they were going to get out of this alive, and damn it, so were Roger and Samantha. I hadn't vowed many things in my life, but I was vowing this.

We continued speeding down the road, kicking up clouds of dirt in our path. This is what I'd always envisioned driving a limo to be like.

Because of the way my screwed-up mind works, I thought of several amusing and insensitive comments to make about our current situation, but I didn't think they would be taken in the "mental defense mechanism" spirit in which they were intended, so I kept them to myself.

I had to keep slowing down around corners because of potential tire shredders, but apart from that we were making great time.

And then, up ahead, was a semi truck. The back of it didn't contain a helpful sign reading "Looney Cyborg Makers, Inc." but I was pretty sure this was a good development. Now I just had to hope my friends were inside.

The semi was going fast, but the limo could go faster and I drove up right behind it, doing about fifty.

Now what?

"Helen, I need you up front," I said. "You'll have to drive."

"Why?"

"Because I'm getting out."

Helen climbed over into the front, wincing in pain as she bashed her injured foot against the seat in the process.

I didn't want to let the semi out of my sight, but I also didn't want to do something dumb like crash in the middle of a tricky driver-switch maneuver, so I applied the brakes gently enough to avoid catapulting Theresa onto the floor and brought the limousine to a stop. Helen and I switched spots, and then we took off after the semi again.

"What exactly are you planning to do?" Helen asked.

"I'm getting onto the semi."

"How?"

"Still working that out."

"Andrew, you don't even know if they're in there!"

"They're either in there or they were in the explosion. I'm just trying to hope for the best."

It took about a minute to catch up to the semi. I wasn't sure if the occupants knew they were being followed.

"Get as close behind it as you can without actually ramming it," I instructed.

"You're not going to jump, are you?"

"Still working that out. But yes."

"No!"

"I'm not letting Roger die in there! You have no idea what they're doing to people, even their own people. They're turning them into cyborgs."

"I beg your pardon?"

"Cyborgs. Half-human, half-machine."

"I know what cyborgs are, I just mean...I beg your pardon?"

"I'll explain it later." I rolled down the passenger-side window. "Okay, I'm going to climb out on top of the limo and then out onto the front hood. When you get close enough to the semi, I'm going to jump onto the back."

"Andrew, that's crazy!"

"I don't have any choice!"

"Sure you do." Helen applied the brakes. "Let me stop the car, and *then* you can get on the hood."

"Oh. Yeah. That's much better. Thanks."

When the car stopped, I threw open the passenger door and got out. Joe barked in what I assume was support for my cause. "Make sure the kids know never, ever to do this," I said, shutting the door and climbing onto the front hood.

Helen resumed driving. None of the insane things I'd done in my life up to this point including jumping from moving vehicles, so it would be nice to add a new experience to my résumé.

It wasn't long before we caught up to the semi again. I inched my way closer to the edge of the front hood, not feeling particularly secure in my balance. I hoped my missing pinky wouldn't be a liability.

I waved for Helen to move closer to the semi. Now about two feet separated the two vehicles. If the driver of the semi suddenly decided to slam on his brakes, I was going to be extraordinarily squished.

Okay, you'll be fine, I told myself. *You can do this. You've seen it in hundreds of movies. The only thing those actors have that you don't are stunt doubles and CGI effects.*

Helen got closer. I moved into a squatting position, promptly lost my balance, and very nearly took a dive right off the front of the limousine. I managed to steady myself and recover from my heart attack, and then I got myself back into the squatting position.

It really wasn't that bad of a jump. Hell, if she got any closer, I could just step across. No problem. Piece of cake.

And then either the semi slowed down or Helen sped up. The front of the limousine hit the back of the semi, not hard enough to do any damage but hard enough to give the limo one hell of a jolt.

I tumbled backwards, breaking my fall with my hands. I'd never ridden in a semi truck before, so I didn't know for sure, but I assumed they'd be able to feel a limousine ramming into their back.

I glanced back at Helen. She looked apologetic.

The semi didn't seem to be slowing down or swerving or anything, so I got back into my jumping position. If they knew we were back here, it was even more crucial than ever that I get Roger and Samantha to safety as quickly as possible.

Helen brought me closer to the rear of the semi again. I took a deep breath, imagined myself as Indiana Jones or James Bond or even a Buster Keaton instead of the Stan Laurel that I really was, and made the leap.

Chapter Twenty-Three

Making the jump onto the semi was surprisingly easy. Almost too easy, making me think that perhaps the back half of the semi was going to topple over and crush me.

Now, the big question was, if I were a hostage in this semi truck, where would I be? If Roger and Samantha were up front, that was going to force me to climb up onto the semi's roof, crawl to the front, and do some sort of daring maneuver to get into the front seat, after which I'd probably get shot. Hopefully they weren't up front.

I'd check the back first. It was closer.

We sped past a faded wooden sign reading "Wreitzer Park." Though I only got a quick glance, I had to admit the place looked pretty nice. Savage killers notwithstanding, Samantha had made a good choice.

I crouched down, not having much room to crouch, and grabbed the handle that unlatched the sliding rear door.

It wouldn't budge. I pulled as hard as I could, but the handle held firm. I noticed a keyhole in the lower corner of the door. Damn.

Helen had fallen back, so I waved for her to drive closer again, and then motioned for her to roll down her window. "I need the keys!" I shouted.

Helen stuck her head out the window. "What?"

"Keys!" I made a key-turning-in-a-lock motion. "I need Medusa's keys!"

I wasn't sure if Helen knew who Medusa was, but she nodded her understanding and went to work, presumably detaching the limo key from the rest of the keys on the ring.

She held up the key ring. "Throw it!" I shouted, reaching out with one hand while holding on to the semi with the other.

Helen got as close to the semi as she could without ramming it again, and then tossed me the keys.

I caught them.

And then they bounced out of my hand.

I lunged for them, momentarily losing sight of the fact that I was hanging off the back of a speeding semi truck, and fell forward. I caught the keys as I fell and both of my hands slammed onto the front hood of the limousine.

Now I was stuck between the two vehicles in a push-up position. Nice.

We hit a bump, and my feet slipped off the back of the semi. My shoes scraped the ground, and for a second I was terrified I was going to be pulled underneath the limo.

Helen quickly slowed down.

My shoes scraped against the dirt road a few more times as I frantically struggled to climb all the way up onto the hood of the limo. With the keys in my right hand I couldn't get a solid grip, and my hand slid down the front hood, scraping the paint job along the way.

I let go of the keys and got a better grip. As the keys slid toward me, I slammed my face against the hood and caught them in my teeth.

I got my feet back safely on the hood and gave Helen a thumbs-up sign. She gave me an incredulous look.

She picked up speed again, and I did another leap onto the back of the semi. I bent down, took the key ring out of my mouth, and tested the first key of about fifteen.

Nope.

I tested the second key.

Nope.

I noticed she had a keychain depicting Medusa from *Clash of the Titans*. Cool.

The third key didn't work, either.

The semi took a sharp turn that forced me to grab hold with both hands, but I didn't drop the keys. The woods were thinning to my left, and I realized we were about to enter the freeway.

The semi picked up speed. I regained my balance and tried the fourth key. Nope.

The fifth, sixth, and seventh keys didn't work, either.

The eighth key slid in perfectly.

And then broke off in the lock when I turned it.

The semi merged onto the freeway and picked up speed.

I tried to turn what was left of the key, but there was no way that was going to work with just my fingers. I needed pliers or tweezers or nail clippers.

Helen probably had nail clippers.

I motioned for her to drive up close again. I leapt back onto the front hood, ignoring the horrified expression of the elderly woman in a red Saturn next to us, and crawled up to the windshield.

"Fingernail clippers!" I shouted.

She picked up a red purse from the seat and tossed it into the back, saying something to Kyle I couldn't hear. I waited less-than-patiently for a few moments, and then Kyle passed something up to Helen. She reached out the window and handed the fingernail clippers to me.

I jumped back onto the semi, feeling like a professional at this point.

We had to be doing about seventy by now. If I lost my balance and fell off, I'd be a nice long smear across the pavement.

I opened the fingernail clippers, managed to get them around the broken key, and turned. The key began to turn...slowly...slowly...

Success!

I stuffed the fingernail clippers into my pocket in case I needed to clip somebody with them, and then pulled on the handle to release the sliding door latch. This time it moved.

I grabbed the handle on the door, strained for a few seconds, and then raised the door a couple of feet, hoping all of this hadn't been for nothing.

I pushed it up all the way and was met with a blast of freezing cold air. I looked inside.

Corpses galore.

There were dozens of them. Some were strapped to the walls of the semi, while others dangled from a huge contraption running along the center of the semi like clothing at a dry cleaners.

All of them were cyborgs. There were corpses with guns for hands, corpses with body armor, corpses with flashing lights on their bodies, corpses with robot heads, two corpses welded together like Siamese twins...a huge horrific variety.

Some of them seemed relatively fresh. Others were mostly rotted away.

Troll was running toward me.

I moved out of the way just in time, grabbing onto a cold and clammy dead arm to keep from falling out of the semi.

I ran past the dangling corpses toward the front of the vehicle, which was lit from above. At the far end, my heart leapt as I saw Roger and Samantha, seated side-by-side, strapped to their chairs, both of them alive!

Samantha's face looked unharmed, but her clothing was marked with spots of blood. Lots of them.

"How stupid can you be?" Troll demanded from behind me. I spun around and saw him coming toward me with his trusty knife. "You could've been home free. Let me tell you, buddy, I spent some quality time with that bitch, and she's not worth saving."

I clenched my fists.

Troll rushed at me again. I pushed through a pair of dangling corpses into the aisle on the other side then quickly looked around for something to use as a weapon.

Well, hell, there were plenty of possibilities.

But Troll found one first. He grabbed the wrist of one of the cyborgs and pointed it at me. I ducked back into the row of dangling corpses as a gunshot went off.

These corpses were loaded!

He fired again, hitting the arm of a corpse next to me and sending a squirt of what I assumed was formaldehyde into the air. I grabbed the closest corpse arm, but it was outfitted with a calculator that didn't look especially helpful.

I ran back toward the rear of the vehicle. The limousine was no longer behind us.

I looked over at a corpse strapped to the wall. Half of its face had been hollowed out and replaced with an abnormally large steel-toothed grin. Its eye sockets were empty. Its hand was a small cannon.

Before I could unstrap its arm, I heard the roar of a motor. Troll burst into the aisle, pushing a cyborg corpse on wheels. One of its arms was entirely metal, extended in front of it, and contained a running chainsaw.

Troll rushed toward me at top speed, the chainsaw severing various protruding corpse body parts as it rolled down the aisle.

I pushed my way into the other aisle, watching as the corpse rolled out of the back of the truck and landed on the hood of a Volkswagen behind us. The car swerved away as the chainsaw blade tore through the hood, sending up a shower of sparks.

Troll pushed his way into my aisle. I used a good old fashioned corpse fist to punch him in the face.

"Ooooooh," he said with an excited grin. I really, really hated Troll.

I dove at him and we both hit the floor, inches away from the open rear of the semi. Troll rolled me over, and we found ourselves underneath several dangling corpse feet, one of which had metal shoes lined with razor blades.

We rolled again, into the other aisle. I put my hands tightly around Troll's neck, trying to strangle him. With my luck, the sick freak was into asphyxiation, too.

I squeezed hard, hoping his eyes would pop right out of their sockets.

I'd forgotten he still had his knife, but I saw the flash of the blade an instant before it would have plunged into my side. I released his neck and rolled off of him. Troll slammed the knife toward me, the tip striking the floor of the semi.

I kicked him in the face with a corpse foot.

Troll got up and quickly began to unfasten another dangling corpse. I took that opportunity to push back into the other aisle and hurry toward Roger and Samantha. "Any suggestions?" I asked.

They both shook their heads.

Troll appeared at the end of our aisle, holding a corpse in his arms. Well, half a corpse. This one was gone from the waist down. It had been a woman. Her hands were comprised of several blades, each about half a foot long, arranged like propellers.

The blades began to spin.

I reached over and unfastened the nearest corpse, which dropped into my arms and was a hell of a lot heavier than I expected. I managed to keep it in an upright position, and slid it down the aisle toward Troll.

Its head lolled back, looking at me upside-down. I pushed its head forward again.

"Cyborg corpse fight!" Troll shouted gleefully. I lifted my corpse's arm, which was a standard-issue dead arm, and tried to punch him with it. The arm went into the blades and within seconds was gone up to the elbow.

Troll thrust his corpse toward me. The blades ripped through my corpse, chopping through flesh and bone. As the blades came through to the other side I released my hold on my useless cadaver and got the hell out of the way.

Troll cackled with laughter, but stopped as he realized my corpse was wedged on one of the blades. He had to put both bodies on the floor and brace mine with his foot to get the blades out. They popped free with a shower of embalming fluid.

I made a move toward the other side, but realized that Troll's next act might be to use the blades on Roger and Samantha. I freed another corpse, this one with metal plating on its torso.

It was way too heavy to keep upright and I dropped it to the floor. I briefly reflected upon the fact that I was showing some severe disrespect for the dead, and then proceeded to show more disrespect for the dead by unlatching another cyborg.

I pressed a button on its back. An electronic voice boomed: "Suicide sequence initiated. Twenty seconds to self-destruct."

"Get it out of here!" Troll screamed. "I'll help you!"

Together we dragged the corpse to the rear of the semi. Two cars were behind us. "Get the hell out of the way!" I shouted, waving for them to move.

The cars moved.

We tossed the corpse out the back. It exploded as soon as it struck the pavement, sending body bits twenty feet into the air and covering the automobiles in the other lane.

"Don't press any more buttons," Troll told me.

"I won't."

Troll tackled me, and we smashed into one of the corpses still strapped to the wall.

"Suicide sequence initiated," boomed an identical electronic voice. "Self-destruct in twenty seconds."

"Get it out of here! Get it out of here!" Troll shouted. We hurriedly unfastened the straps, dragged the corpse to the edge, and shoved it over the side.

That explosion was red and much more disgusting. Apparently it was a fresher corpse that hadn't been embalmed. A nearby car's windshield was drenched, and the vehicle scraped against the center divider for a few seconds until the driver regained control.

Out of the corner of my eye, I noticed Goblin strapped to the wall, next to the corpse with the hollowed-out face.

I punched Troll in the chin. "Are any more of these rigged to explode?"

"Six, I think."

I punched him again, knocking him back several steps. Then I grabbed the cannon hand of the corpse with the hollowed-out face, took aim at Troll, and pulled the trigger.

A huge stream of flame jettisoned from the cannon, missing Troll but hitting an entire row of the dangling corpses. As their dead bodies caught on fire and the back of the semi began to fill with smoke, I decided this had probably been another one of my less-than-completely-desirable moves.

Chapter Twenty-Four

Helen's Side

After Andrew made it inside the semi, I swerved into the next lane and sped up alongside the front of the truck. The driver looked down at me and nervously stroked his goatee.

I wasn't quite sure what to do at this point. It wasn't like I could ram the semi off the road. The best I could do is keep up with it and be ready to help out when it finally came to a stop, or when Andrew (and hopefully Roger and Samantha) were ready to jump back onto the hood of the limousine.

I hated feeling so useless, but what else could I do?

"Kyle, how's your sister?" I asked.

"She's breathing funny."

"Theresa, can you hear me? How do you feel?"

"I hurt..." Theresa groaned, so softly I could barely hear her.

"It's okay, sweetie. We're going to get you help. I promise." I tilted the rear-view mirror so I could see her. "You're being very brave. I'm very proud of you."

This news didn't seem to make Theresa feel any better.

I reached over and picked up the cell phone. If I let the police know exactly where we were, maybe they could—

"Mommy watch out!"

I swerved, slammed on the brakes, and tried to remember if I'd fastened my seat belt. Like a television with its electrical cord yanked from the outlet, my world shut off.

Chapter Twenty-Five

Burning corpses in the back of a semi: Not good.

Not fragrant, either.

Troll was on the side with Roger and Samantha, so I hurried to the front, expecting to find him hovering over them, knife raised, face contorted into a sadistic grin.

Which is exactly what I saw.

But I'd gotten to the point where rushing at a knife-wielding maniac didn't seem like that big of a deal. I grabbed his maniacal knife-wielding arm and slammed him into another of the corpses strapped to the wall. This one didn't inform us that it would be self-destructing.

The semi swerved abruptly, knocking Troll and I back into the aisle with the burning corpses. Sparks were flying from several of them.

"You've ruined it all!" Troll shouted. "Mr. Burke is gonna shit a brick sideways!"

He slashed at me with the knife, missing completely. The smoke was starting to burn my eyes and it had to be affecting Troll as well because his next two slashes were even further off the mark.

He screamed in frustration and flung the knife at me. I heard the *thunk* of the blade hitting dead flesh behind me.

Troll coughed.

The flames were growing larger and more intense. Letting Roger and Samantha burn to death after all of this was simply not an option.

I let out a howl of primal rage, or what I figured was primal rage, and ran at Troll. I punched him in the face with my good hand and then my bad hand, not even feeling the pain.

Troll seemed to enjoy the first punch. The second punch, not so much.

I punched again and again, doing the primal rage howl thing with each one. I pummeled him with force I didn't even realize existed inside of me.

Troll spat out a large mouthful of blood. "Truce...?"

I grabbed him by the collar and rushed down the aisle, dragging him along the burning corpses as I did so. This son of a bitch was taking a leap out of the back of a speeding semi. Troll cried out in protest and struggled, but he couldn't get away.

As we reached the edge at a high rate of speed, I let him go.

No witty comment was necessary.

But Troll didn't fly out onto the pavement as planned. As he fell, his foot wedged behind one of the metal steps and he pitched forward onto the freeway.

He tried to use his hands to break his fall. It was not pretty. Troll found himself being dragged face-down behind a semi going about seventy, and not much more needs to be said about that.

There were no cars behind us to witness the gory sight. Presumably a smoke-billowing semi truck was not something other drivers wanted to linger around.

I returned to the back, wincing as a particularly nasty shower of sparks got me in the arm. I could now barely see Roger and Samantha through the smoke, but I felt my way over then removed Samantha's gag.

"Are you okay?" I asked her, as I began to unfasten the straps.

"Better than I was ten seconds ago."

"I don't know if this will help," I said, "but Troll's face is currently marking out a new lane divider."

"Actually, that does help."

"Good."

After I got her free, I went to work on Roger. "I bet you thought I wasn't coming back for you," I said.

"No, I thought you'd be here sooner."

"Sorry. I got distracted."

"What happened after they took you away?"

I stabbed my daughter and had a great time doing it...

"Nothing."

Samantha helped me unstrap Roger from his chair, and before long they were both free. Roger scooped Samantha up in his arms and the three of us quickly moved to the open end of the semi. The fire had spread and now included all of the hanging corpses in the center.

"I'm, uh, sure you've got a splendid escape plan," said Roger.

I knelt down, yanked Troll's foot out from where it was wedged, and set what was left of his body free. "You haven't had anything to do for the past few minutes. Didn't you think of one?"

"Extend the ramp," said Samantha.

I unlatched the metal ramp and Roger and I pushed it out to its full length. It scraped against the pavement with a sound even more hideous than the smell of burning flesh.

"This isn't going to work," Roger insisted. "Even without the fall, if we hit the pavement going this fast we'll be killed!"

"Well, we can't stay in here!" I said, gesturing to the burning corpses. Where the hell was Helen when I needed a limo to leap upon?

One of the corpses exploded behind us, causing several others to drop to the floor.

"This whole truck could blow up!" Samantha shouted.

"We can get off this thing," I said. "We just need some kind of padding."

"What kind of padding?" Roger asked.

I looked over at the corpses strapped to the wall.

Roger shook his head. "Oh, no way!"

I stood up and began to unfasten the corpse of a heavyset male with crossbows for hands and numerous wires protruding from his skin. "You look for some fluffy pillows. I'll take down the dead guy."

Instead of arguing, Roger helped me unfasten the corpse. "Oh, jeez, this is gonna be sick."

"At least they're not maggoty."

"Shut up. I mean it."

"Samantha, Goblin is hanging up on the other side. Try to tear off his feet."

"Say what?"

"They're wheels! Do it!"

Samantha nodded and left, scooting along on her knees.

"This is wrong on so many levels," said Roger, as we released the body. It fell to the floor, landing on its belly. Pushing as hard as we could, we managed to shove it over to the ramp.

"Here they are." Samantha handed me Goblin's foot-wheels. I slammed one of the bloody spikes between the heavyset corpse's shoulder blades and another into its lower back.

"We need more," I said, pointing to one of the fallen corpses. "That one has wheels, too."

Roger hurried over to it and tried to pry off the feet. "They won't come off! There's a metal band around them!" He glanced around and lifted the arm of another corpse. Its hand was a hacksaw. "You probably don't want to see this."

Moments later he returned. I pulled the meat off the wheels and tossed it aside, and then slammed the next two spikes into the corpse's back.

Another explosion, this one spraying us extremely well.

The semi swerved violently and dangling burning corpse legs just narrowly missed my head.

"Let's turn him over!" Roger, Samantha, and I all turned the corpse onto its back, and then maneuvered it over to the top of the ramp, head-first. It didn't roll easily.

"No way in hell is this going to work," said Roger.

"It'll be fine," I insisted. "We'll just all hold on tight and go for a ride. You take the front, Roger."

Roger climbed onto the corpse and sat on its chest.

"Oh, God...oh, God..." he said. "I can think of so many things I'd rather be doing right now."

The semi swerved again, and Samantha and I momentarily lost our hold on the corpse.

It was long enough. The corpse rolled down the ramp as Roger frantically turned himself around and tried to reach for my arm.

"Shiiiiiit!" he cried, as the corpse rolled off the ramp and onto the freeway. Two of the wheels immediately went flying in opposite directions. Roger pressed himself down against the body as it slid across the pavement, its head bouncing up and down and its arms flapping.

The other two wheels popped out from underneath the corpse, but it continued to slide. Roger remained on top.

As the corpse slowed and we sped away, I could see Roger was going to be fine.

Samantha and I were still screwed, though.

"Y'know, call me optimistic, but I think Corpse Surfing is going to be the next big fad to sweep the nation," I said.

Samantha just gaped at me.

"It worked, though, didn't it?" I asked. "So let's just find another cyborg and some more wheels and get the hell out of here, too!"

The semi turned slightly as we went off an exit. This could either be really good or really bad, depending on whether or not Mr. Burke decided to slow down to a reasonable speed or to just plow through everything doing seventy.

Since I didn't detect any reduction in speed, it appeared the latter was going to be the case.

"If we die," said Samantha, "I just want you to know I've always felt you were a really great person. Roger is lucky to have you as a friend."

"I've always felt the same way about you, too," I said, somewhat annoyed that my potential final words on this earth had to be a little white lie.

We took down another corpse. This one wasn't as big as the first and was unlikely to provide as much padding, but we had to make do with what we had. And with the thick smoke and dangerous flames, we also wouldn't be finding any more wheels.

There was a huge jolt as the semi smashed through something. A moment later I saw it had been a thick wooden fence.

The pavement turned to grass.

The semi began to slow down.

We were saved! Even without a handy corpse for protection, we certainly could handle a jump onto grass. What were a few more bumps, bruises, and open wounds at this point?

I saw Mr. Burke rolling on the grass, obviously just having leapt out of the vehicle. That probably wasn't good.

Another huge jolt.

And then suddenly our view of the grass became a view of the clear blue sky as the semi tilted at a forty-five degree angle.

Chapter Twenty-Six

Samantha and I slid to the back of the semi, past the burning bodies, and smacked into the rear wall. The ramp dropped back into its chute with a loud crash.

The tilt of the semi increased. We hurriedly pressed ourselves into the corner as the burning bodies that had fallen slid down the floor toward us. I held on to the leg of the corpse strapped to the wall next to me and kicked the bodies away from us.

"It's okay, no problem," I said. "We're just hanging over a cliff or something."

The dangling corpses above us were swinging violently back and forth, and burning debris fluttered down upon us. It hurt to look up through the smoke and I launched into a fit of uncontrollable coughing.

As Samantha tried to crawl up the slope, the tilt increased yet again, creating an almost vertical climb, and she tumbled back against the far wall.

"It's okay, really," I insisted, when I could speak again. "They've got to have helicopters around, or maybe Roger flagged somebody down who has a rope, or maybe—"

"Andrew, stop trying to make the best of this!"

One of the hanging corpses came loose. It dropped and hit the far wall with a *thud* that caused the semi to shift a few inches.

"We can still get out of this! We can...we can...we can climb the bodies!"

"What?"

"We can climb up the bodies that are strapped to the wall!"

"I can't!"

"Yes, you can! I'll be right behind you." I grabbed her hand and placed it on the waist of the closest cyborg.

Another body fell. This one felt like it knocked the semi back a couple of feet. A couple of rounds of what sounded like automatic weapon fire went off as it hit, but I didn't feel any new holes in my body.

Samantha pulled herself up onto the corpse and I stayed behind her, trying to hold her steady. She screamed as she used her mangled foot to push herself up. I was worried the noise might have an avalanche effect and send the semi over whatever precipice it was hanging over, but I figured she couldn't help it.

She climbed up onto the second body in the cyborg ladder. I followed.

Two bodies fell at once. The impact jolted the semi enough that I let out a scream of my own, but we both held on to the corpses and continued climbing.

"You know, people pay good money to go mountain climbing on vacation," I said, hoping my sparkling wit would distract her from her agony and terror. "This is a lot better. This is going to be the new ride at Universal Studios." Samantha didn't tell me to shut up, so I figured that was a good sign.

Then she grabbed a cyborg part that wasn't meant to have somebody climbing on it. It came loose and she lost her grip. She fell down to my corpse, grabbed it, failed to hang on, and crashed to the bottom.

"That's okay," I said. "Let's just try it again."

She didn't respond, and I could barely see her through the smoke. What if she'd broken her neck?

I climbed down and knelt down next to her. "C'mon, Samantha, you can do this."

She shook her head. "No, I can't. He tortured me...I mean, he really...his knife...I just can't do it. I've got nothing left. Get out of here. Please."

"Not without you."

"You can't carry me! Please, we don't both need to die here."

"Look, I don't have time to get into the details, but one of the few possibilities for me getting a happy ending out of this is for me to bring you safely back to the love of your life. So we're getting out of this together. Don't argue."

"How are we going to do it if I can't climb?"

I considered that.

"I don't know. I'm still sort of hoping we'll be rescued."

The semi shifted and moved back at least two more feet.

"Maybe it's a really tiny cliff," I said. "We may be stressing out over nothing."

"Yeah, I'm sure Mr. Burke jumped out so he could drive the semi over a really tiny cliff."

"Don't be so pessimistic."

"Sorry."

"If we can't climb, we'll just have to..."

I left that sentence unfinished for a long moment.

Fly out? Teleport out? Wake up from a bad dream?

Shoot our way out?

Which of the corpses was it that nearly shot my foot off when it fell? I searched through the burning bodies as well as I could, yelping in pain about eight times, and found an arm with a machine gun on the end. Sweet.

I also found an axe with which to lop it off.

I did so quickly. Then I picked up the machine gun, let out my ninth yelp, and dropped it. The damn thing was *hot*.

"Sorry about this," I told Samantha as I took off my shoes and jeans. The next time Kyle questioned that whole "Make sure you have on clean underwear" parental command, I'd have an anecdote to share with him.

Using my jeans to keep my hands from getting burnt off, I picked up the machine gun, pointed it at the wall of the semi, and pulled the trigger.

The semi was filled with a deafening *ratatatatatatat* of machine gun fire and clangs as the bullets struck metal. Streaks of light burst through the holes.

I hate to admit it, but standing there wearing only my underwear, firing a machine gun, made me feel *incredibly* macho.

The bullets continued to chew away at the semi wall.

The semi began to slide backward.

I kept firing, hoping nobody was on the other side (unless it was Mr. Burke).

The machine gun finally ran out of bullets and I tossed it aside. We now had a really scary-looking opening with jagged edges that didn't look large enough to climb out without slicing ourselves to ribbons, but, hey, beggars can't be choosers.

The semi was still sliding. I looked through the hole and saw that we were indeed dangling over a cliff, that it was an extremely long drop to the ground, but that we'd smashed through a metal fence that was now twisted and within our reach. "You first," I told Samantha.

She wasted no time. She crawled over to the hole and I quickly helped her through, removing a long strip of her left leg in the process. She grabbed hold of the fence and began to scoot toward solid ground.

The semi slid again, taking the fence out of my reach.

I frantically began to climb the corpses.

"Andrew!" I heard Samantha scream on the other side.

I didn't respond because that would have used up valuable climbing energy. I tried to think happy thoughts. Happy climby thoughts.

I climbed up the third, fourth, and fifth bodies. Only about a dozen left. No problem.

As I got about halfway there, the semi began to pick up speed. So did I.

Helen, Theresa, Kyle, Roger, and Samantha were all alive, and damn it, I was going to join them. I climbed as fast as I could, eyes feeling like they were sizzling from the smoke, lungs burning, but not stopping.

I reached the second-to-last corpse.

Don't lose your grip. Don't lose your grip. Don't grab anything detachable. Don't grab anything detachable.

I reached for the top corpse, accidentally stuck my hand in its open, screaming mouth, but pulled myself up anyway.

And then I was at the top.

And then the semi fell over the edge of the cliff.

And then I jumped.

The semi smashed into the riverbank about a hundred feet below. I hung from the cliff face, holding nothing that felt remotely firm enough to sustain me. My fingers dug into the grass but I could tell I was seconds away from a nice long fall onto a semi filled with burning cyborg corpses.

Samantha thrust her hand at me. I grabbed it.

As she pulled, I tried to use my feet against the dirt cliff face to give myself some leverage. It wasn't really working. But since I hadn't died in all of the other times I'd vowed I wouldn't die, I sure wasn't going to die here.

With Samantha's help, I pulled myself most of the way onto solid ground.

In the distance I saw Mr. Burke limping toward us.

I was pretty sure he was holding a gun.

"Samantha! Watch out!"

A shot rang out.

I tasted several drops of Samantha's blood in my open mouth.

And then I fell.

Chapter Twenty-Seven

Helen's Side

I opened my eyes to red and blue flashing lights.

"Where are my children?" I demanded, sitting up in a panic. I was on a stretcher.

"It's okay, they're both in the ambulance," the paramedic assured me.

"My daughter was stabbed! You have to help her!"

"It's under control. You've been in an accident, but the other driver wasn't hurt, so just relax."

"I can't relax! My husband, have you seen him?"

"Ma'am, there wasn't anybody else in the vehicle."

"I know! He was in a semi."

The paramedic's eyes widened. "Okay, we've got police cars investigating that right now. But there's nothing you can do, so just relax." He gave me an injection. "Just relax."

Chapter Twenty-Eight

So here's what happened.

I didn't plummet down onto the semi, shattering my bones into a million pieces and burning my flesh in the flames within. Instead I slid down the cliff face, scraping the hell out of my arms and chest, and managed to get myself steadied about halfway down.

It was way too steep to climb back up without the aid of a corpse ladder, so I was forced to stay there, helpless, until I heard vehicles approach overhead.

When the cops pulled me to safety, they were loading Samantha into an ambulance. I hurried over there as best I could, trying to see if she was dead.

She'd been hit in the shoulder.

Mr. Burke was nowhere to be seen.

I let them load me into the ambulance.

As we sped down the freeway, the paramedic gave me the news. Helen, Theresa, and Kyle were all being rushed to the nearest hospital. They were all alive.

Roger was also in an ambulance on his way to the same hospital.

"Will she be okay?" I asked, looking over at Samantha.

The paramedic nodded. "She'll live. But what on earth *happened* to you people?"

I didn't answer.

❧❧

Roger got released first, and his job was to bring us huge amounts of fast food instead of the crap they had available at the hospital.

Samantha regained consciousness in the middle of the second night. I got the news while I was sitting in Theresa's room, staring at my daughter, hating myself.

Kyle sat in the room with me, his arm bandaged up. "She's going to wake up," he said, knowingly.

"Yes, she will."

He scooted his chair closer to mine. "I know you didn't mean to do it. I know they gave you drugs."

"You're right," I said. "They did."

"I'm never, ever, ever going to use drugs."

I managed a smile. "Good for you, kiddo."

He looked at me, his expression solemn. "Daddy, if you want to cry, it's okay. I promise I won't tell anybody."

I held him tight and did just that.

Theresa regained consciousness three days later and couldn't remember anything that happened.

~~*

"Mr. Burke got away. He must have hitchhiked or stolen a car at gunpoint, but as I write this the police still haven't caught him. I've got this unpleasant feeling that he'll be showing up again, but personally, I hope right now he's making cyborgs in hell."

~~*

Witch was found sitting on the side of the road, muttering incoherently to herself. The last I heard, she still hadn't spoken to anybody at the psychiatric ward.

~~*

Most of the corpses were identified by their dental records, at least those who still had teeth. They'd been missing over a period of three years.

Roger had ridden to safety on a man named Herschel Eberhardt, whose family issued a statement saying how proud they were that Herschel had saved a life six months after his death.

~~*

Samantha wouldn't tell us exactly what Troll did to her behind the closed door in the lab, but of course the doctors told us about her injuries. You don't want to know. Trust me.

~~*

The doctors admitted there wasn't much they could do to reattach a finger that had been flushed down the toilet. I kept trying to encourage a cool nickname like "Nine-Finger Mayhem," but nobody embraced that idea.

~~*

Joe was perfectly fine.

~~*

A few days later, Samantha and Theresa were transferred back to Chamber Memorial Hospital. And two weeks after the whole ordeal began, we had a huge "Welcome Home!" party for Theresa, which included balloons, cake, pug tricks, and fun for the entire family.

Helen stroked my arm tenderly as we sat on the couch, watching Theresa and Kyle fight over who loved Joe the most. I'd apologized to her approximately 1,837,612 times for what I'd done, and after a couple of days she seemed convinced I wouldn't have a relapse.

That night, we lay in bed, sweaty from our lovemaking. It was the first time we'd had sex since before the vacation, and though we were forced to be extremely careful because of our injuries, it had been a wonderfully pleasant experience, even with that stupid pug scraping on the door the entire time.

"I love you so much," she whispered. "I don't want to ever lose you."

"You won't." I kissed her gently on the lips. "I promise."

Theresa screamed.

I threw on a bathrobe and we rushed into her bedroom. Theresa was sitting up in bed, sobbing.

"What's the matter, sweetie? What's wrong?" asked Helen.

"Daddy! Daddy's trying to kill me!"

⁓⁓

I lay on Roger's couch, unable to get comfortable. His couch sucked. Quite frankly, his apartment sucked, too. He needed to just move in with Samantha already. She had a much nicer place.

His cat, Reverse Snowflake, jumped up onto my chest and began to lick my face. "Your cat has very foul breath," I informed Roger as he walked into the living room.

"That's only because he pukes a lot."

I sat up and Roger sat down on the couch next to me. "What time is it?" I asked.

"Middle of the night."

"That's what I figured."

"Samantha told me all about what happened in the back of the semi."

"You mean when I took off my pants?"

"No, when you wouldn't leave without her."

"Oh, that. I was drunk."

"It means a lot to me. I'm serious."

"Well, you would've done the same for Helen."

"Yeah, I probably would have. So I guess we're even." He grinned. "Anyway, thanks for getting her out of there."

"No problem."

"So is it okay if she hangs out with us at the Java Joint next Wednesday?"

"Sure."

"I'm kidding, Andrew."

"Oh. Good."

"Get some sleep."

"I will."

I lay back down and closed my eyes. I still couldn't sleep, so I pushed the cat away, got up, found a notebook, and started writing.

And now I'm just about done.

It felt good to write this all down, but I'm not sure I want anybody to read it, except for Helen, who filled in some of the gaps.

I'm going to lock it away with instructions not to publish it until after I'm dead.

Or maybe I'll publish it after I get a happier ending.

So if you're reading these words...well, let's pretend it's the latter. I'm feeling optimistic.

Epilogue

Helen and I gazed up at the sonogram monitor, which featured bizarre shapes that looked like nothing identifiable as a human or even alien child. The sight brought tears to our eyes anyway.

She'd taken a beating, but she hadn't lost the baby. She was one strong mother and she was going to have one strong kid.

"Is it a boy or girl?" Helen asked.

The doctor smiled. "Both."

My eyes widened. "Oh my God! The kid's a hermaphrodite?"

Helen laughed and playfully swatted my arm. "No, you goof. He means we're having twins." The realization of that fact quickly sunk in and her voice became somewhat less chipper. "Twins."

"Actually, no," said the doctor. "Triplets."

Helen swatted my arm again. This time it wasn't quite as playful.

Printed in the United States
44693LVS00007B/244-252